T0353649

# BANGALORS

## Dragon War

*Carl E. Boyett*

authorHOUSE®

*AuthorHouse™*
*1663 Liberty Drive*
*Bloomington, IN 47403*
*www.authorhouse.com*
*Phone: 833-262-8899*

*Published by AuthorHouse  09/23/2024*

*ISBN: 979-8-8230-3441-8 (sc)*
*ISBN: 979-8-8230-3440-1 (e)*

*Library of Congress Control Number: 2024920738*

*Print information available on the last page.*

# CONTENTS

||||||||||||||||||||||||||||||||||||||||||||

# CHAPTER 1
||||||||||||||||||||||||||||||||||||||||||||||||
# THE ERIDANI NEBULA

Caalin had briefed his crew on the mission they had for the Eridani Nebula and everyone was preparing for the jump. Caalin took his seat and gave the command to engineering, "Prepare to jump, destination the Eridani Nebula." Dargon turned to Caalin and showed him the hologram again, "Caalin it looks like there is an asteroid field that moves in and out of the Nebula, we could use that to hide the ship from their sensors." Caalin looked at the hologram, "You're right that is a great idea." He then told to Ssam, "Get us as close to the asteroid field as possible then ease us into it, we will use it for cover."

Ssam quickly made the adjustment and said, "Changes have been made we are ready to jump on your command." Caalin then announced to the entire ship, "We are jumping to the Eridani Nebula in ten seconds so prepare your selves." Ssam counted down the time then shouted, "Jumping now!" There was a flash and they were now in a dimensional jump and Ssam reported, "We will be at the edge of the asteroid field in fifteen minutes." Caalin replied, "Great once we are there ease us in as far as you can without damaging the ship please." Ssam Laughed, "We will do our best Captain."

Soon they were out of the jump and slowly moving into the asteroid field. Caalin spotted a large asteroid in front of them and called down to engineering, "Mouse can you scan the larger asteroid in front of us and tell me if it has any iron deposits in it?" Mouse quickly ran a scan and came back, "It looks like it is seventy percent iron." Caalin smiled, "That will do fine; navigation land us on that asteroid, engineering once we have landed, magnetically lock us down on it." He looked over at Dargon, "This will be our base of operations and they will not know we are here."

Caalin stood up, "Dargon you and Ssam come with me, Clair get your team and meet us in the briefing room." He then called to the medical team and engineering, "Ang I need you and Mouse to meet me in the briefing room." After a few minutes everyone was assembled in the briefing room waiting to hear what Caalin had in mind. When they arrived Caalin had the map of the Nebula up and had highlighted the three planets they needed to check out.

Caalin look over to Clair, "I will need two of your people to go with me, and you pick them." He turned to Dargon, "I am leaving you in charge of the ship so be on alert in case we need your help." He Smiled at Ang, "You are our medical person in case someone is injured." Then he looked over to Mouse and Ssam, "Mouse we need you just in case we need to get inside any locked doors and Ssam's job is to get us down to the planets unseen." Ssam shook his head, "How did I know that was the only reason I was selected." Mouse patted him on the shoulder, "Well at less you are not just a lock pick." They both chuckle at the comment then Caalin cleared his throat and they stopped.

Clair looked over at her team and thought for a moment then said, "Faelara and Aeron the two of you will accompany Captain Matthews on this mission or do either of you wish not to go, if so speak up now." The two of them quickly stated they were willing to go on the mission. Caalin smiled, "Fine, everyone collect whatever gear you will need and meet me in the cargo bay in ten minutes." He then turned to Faelara and Aeron, "Will the two of you pull weapons for everyone and bring them along; hopefully we will not need them."

Ten minutes later the away team was now in the cargo bay where the six shuttles were located and they were numbered AS1-S1 and AS1-S2 the two eight person shuttles while AS1-S3, AS1-S4, AS1-S5, and AS1-S6 were the fifteen person shuttles. Caalin told everyone to load their gear onto AS1-S1 and prepare to depart for Corincas since it was the closest planet they would check it out first. As everyone boarded the shuttle Caalin turned to Dargon and Clair, "Take care of our ship if anything happens jump out of here and contact Alliance Headquarters." Dargon smiled at him, "I will do that, but you take care of your team and we will see you when you get back safely."

Caalin smiled as he turned to head for the shuttle, "Keep communications down to a minimum we don't want them to know we are here." Once on the shuttle he moved up to the pilots seat with Ssam seated next to him, "OK pal once we clear the asteroids I need you to make us invisible are you ready?" Ssam looked over at him, "I am always ready so let's get moving." The shuttle lifted off the deck and slowly exited the ship, and then they made their way through the asteroids coming out just inside the nebula. Caalin looked over to Ssam, "It's on you now." Ssam placed his hand on the bulkhead of the shuttle and it disappeared from sight as they made their way toward Corincas.

Soon they were entering the atmosphere of Corincas and making their way down to the planet. Caalin spotted a large cave big enough to land the shuttle in so he slowly moved it inside and set it down. Once on the ground he told everyone, "We will use this as our base of operations and move out from here, Aeron and I will do the recon while the rest of you stay here and watch the shuttle for now. If we locate anything we will come back and fill you in on what we plan to do."

Ang looked over at Caalin, "I can fly as well so maybe I should help the two of you." Caalin smiled at her, "No you are our medical support I need you here just in case you're needed, I couldn't let you get hurt." She lowered her head, "OK I understand, but the two of you had better be careful I don't want any medical work to do while we are here." Before Caalin and Aeron took to flight he looked back over to her, "Well that is the plan, and I hope it is a slow easy going mission." After that he an Aeron took to the air and made their way up to the top of the mountain so they could get a better view of their surroundings.

At the top they stopped and landed on a large flat rock; while Caalin looked around he could see a vase forest with mountain peaks popping up all around. He looked over at Aeron, "Ok we need to stay low to the trees, I want us to space out with about five hundred meters between us that way we can cover more ground. Signal me if you spot anything that looks like it could be a base or outpost." Aeron agreed and the two of them took to the air and flew off along the tree tops looking in all directions.

Back on board the shuttle Mouse got bored waiting on Caalin and Aeron to return so he decided to look around the shuttle, while looking he found a few targeting drones used as targets to test laser systems on ships and shuttles. He thought that while they were gone he would see if he could convert them from targeting drones to scanner drones. Looking further he found a tool kit in one of the other storage compartments

4

then set down with the drones and began working. He worked for a long time, but could not get them to work the way he needed them to because he was missing some of the optical components he needed. He then started going through all the storage compartment looking for more part and came across parts for the shuttle external sensor and cameras used for landing. He took the parts and made his way back to his seat and went back to work. A few hours later he had one drone working the way he wanted it too and decided to take it outside to test it. He walked to the entrance of the cave and released the drone and it started scanning the area as he hoped it would. He had programmed it to go out as far as it could and return after hour of scanning, then as it was returning so were Caalin and Aeron. The drone landed at Mouse's feet and as he was picking it up Caalin and Aeron were landing next to him.

Caalin looked over at Mouse and asked, "What is that you have there?" Mouse smiled, "A drone we can use to scan the planet, but it would be better if we had more of them." Caalin scratched his head, "I am still lost on what you are doing." Mouse replied, "Come with me and lets down load the information from it and I will explain."

The three of them made their way back to the shuttle where Ang was happy to see them and ran out to meet Caalin, "Welcome back, did everything go alright?" Caalin smiled at her, "Good but we can't do this for the entire planet, we can't cover that big of an area." Mouse popped in, "That is why I built this drone, mind you we would need a lot more of them to scan the entire planet but I know we can build them back on the Seeker." Caalin looked at him, "Ok show me the data you have and we will go from there."

Mouse took the drone over to the computer terminal, down loaded the data and showed it to Caalin. The data showed that the drone had gone further and cover ten times the area that Caalin and Aeron were able to cover in just one hour's time. Caalin put his hand on Mouse's shoulder, "So you can build these back on the Seeker?" Mouse smiled, "Yes and all we need to do is land on the planet and release them, I can even make them better than this one with the right parts."

Caalin turned to the group, "Ssam once we are in space let the Seeker know we are on our way back, everyone take your seats we are getting off this planet for now." He then made his way to the pilot's seat and fired up the engines and they slowly rose up off the ground. The ship slowly turned and made its way out of the cave as Caalin told Ssam, "Make us invisible." Ssam placed his hands on the bulkhead and they vanished and made their way upward off the planet. Once in space Ssam sent a coded message to the Seeker to let them know they were headed back.

# CHAPTER 2

|||||||||||||||||||||||||||||||||||||||||||||

# BACK ON THE SEEKER

Caalin maneuvered the shuttle back into the asteroid field and down to where the Seeker set on the large asteroid it was locked onto then slowly brought it to a safe landing in the shuttle bay. As they were leaving the shuttle Caalin told Mouse, "Get all the parts you need then you and the rest of engineering get as many of those drone built that you can; let me know when they are ready." Mouse smiled, "We will get right on it and will have them ready as soon as possible."

As the group exited the shuttle they noticed that everyone was wearing their new uniforms which were a little different depending on who was wearing it. The uniforms were all the same except for the shoulder epaulette, the uniforms had dark grey trousers, with a light grey top, but it seemed that the epaulette color on the shoulders were the same as their old squad colors from Boldoron Academy. It seemed that the former Charlie squad's epaulettes were gold, the Deltas were dark green, and the Beta's were dark blue. Caalin then noticed that everyone that had not attended Boldoron had black epaulettes, and on everyone's epaulettes were their rank insignia. Caalin turned to the group before they dispersed, "It looks like we are out of uniform, I think we should make our way to our rooms and change before going anywhere else."

As Caalin was saying that to the others Marty had walked up to greet them, "Welcome back, I'm glad everyone made it back safely." He smiled, "I could not help overhearing what you just said, so I will let the bridge know you are back onboard and have gone to your rooms to get freshened up." Caalin smiled, "Thanks Marty, can you also have your team resupply the shuttle; I think Mouse has used up a few items in there that need replacing." Marty tipped his head, "We will get right on it."

The away team then made their way to their rooms to get cleaned up and change. When Ang got to her room there on her bed was her new uniform all laid out for her, and on the uniform was a note from Ssophia, "*I thought the group would want to get cleaned up and changed so I laid everyone's uniforms out for them.*" Ang just smiled and made her way to the shower to get cleaned up, thinking to herself about what a good friend she has.

Caalin made his way to the bridge after he had cleaned up and changed into his uniform, once on the bridge he told Asgaya, who was on communications at the time, to call all the officers and advisors up for a quick briefing. Asgaya sent the communications through the ships intercom system and with minutes everyone were assembled in the briefing room.

During the briefing Caalin informed everyone, "It is impossible to search each planet with personnel alone, but thanks to Mouse's ingenuity we have a better plan." He continued, "Mouse and engineering are building drones that can do the job faster than we can, we will take the drone and release them on the planets assigning them areas to scan then retrieve them to process the data." He cleared his throat, "That will be quicker and safer for everyone involved and I think if all goes well we should be able to complete this mission within a weeks time." He then asked, "Does anyone have any questions." Dargon spoke up, "Do you think they will be able to detect the drone as they scan the planet?" Caalin turned to Mouse, "Well since this is your area of expertise I will let you answer that." Mouse smiled, "We are incorporating the technology for the drones to jam and evade any detection." He then looked straight at Dargon, "And I know someone that will be great at assisting with that." Caalin laughed, "Thank you Dargon for volunteering to help, and thank you all for making it here for this briefing; I have to say you all look good in your new uniforms."

Once the meeting was over Caalin joined Ang and headed to the dining hall for something to eat while Mouse and Dargon made their way to engineering to work on the drones. Once in engineering Mouse pulled up the schematics for the drones and began moving parts around while Dargon and Gahe looked for all the parts they would need to convert them. Mouse was finally finished with the design and the other two had pulled all the parts they needed for the job. Mouse had calculated they had enough supplies to build two hundred drones and had reduced the size of the drones to that of a thirty centimeter orb that could change colors to match its surroundings.

Dargon looked at the plans and then at Mouse, "This is going to take us some time to build all of these." Mouse put his hand on Dargon's shoulder, "We only have to build the first few, and the droids we have in a container in the cargo bay will assemble the others." Dargon looked puzzled, "What droids are you talking about?" Mouse smiled, "Follow me." He led Dargon down to the cargo bay and called Marty then asked him, "Will you show us where you put the container that has the androids in it?" Marty led them over to a large container set against the starboard bulkhead, "There you are, but what are you planning to do with them?" Mouse replied, "Activated them and put them to work, what else."

Mouse opened the container and there were ten androids, they were small and almost humanoid in shape. He then walked through activating each one of them and had them exit the container. Mouse looked over at Marty, "Can your guys set up some tables on one side of the shuttle bay as an assembly area, and I need these guys to build some drones for us." Marty replied, "Give us about an hour and we will have it all set up with power and everything you need." Mouse then informed him he would send him a list of parts they would need pulled from storage and placed in the work area.

Dargon looked at Mouse, "OK you have a work force, but how are you going to program all of them to do what we need them to do?" Mouse said, "That is not a problem we just have to program one and it will relay the information to the others." He then had one of the droids he designated as Alpha follow them back to engineering, once they were there he plug Alpha into the computer system and began programming all the need information into the droid.

After programming Alpha they all went down to the shuttle bay and the newly setup work area where Mouse had Alpha transfer the information to all the other droids. After that was completed he had the droid team begin assembling the drones. Mouse turned to Dargon, "When you get back to the bridge you can let Caalin know they should have the drones ready by 10:00 tomorrow." Dragon nodded, "I will relay the message", and then headed back up to the bridge to pass on the information.

After Caalin had the information he had Keyan schedule a 15:00 meeting for the next day with all the officers and the security team to go over their plains for the next trip back to Corincas. Keayan communicated the information to all that would be involved and informed Caalin when it was completed. Caalin then turned it over to Dargon to setup the watch shifts and went to his room to get some rest, it had been quite a day for him.

# CHAPTER 3

||||||||||||||||||||||||||||||||||||||||||||

# MOUSE AND THE VIRERIAN

Mouse had worked late into the night getting the androids working properly on the drones they needed so he decided to stop by the dining hall for something to eat before going to his room to get a little rest. While in the dining hall he ran across Rostrik who ask if he wanted to join him while they ate. Mouse quickly accepted the invitation and took a seat. After a few minutes Rostrik asked Mouse about Captain Matthews, and what type of a person he was. Mouse smiled as he answered the question, "You could not have asked for a better captain for this ship than Caalin, he has been a great friend and he would give his own life if it meant saving someone else's."

Mouse then told Rostrik about things Caalin had done, from saving everyone during the Skyracer race by guiding his ship away from the crowd and getting injured when he ejected, saving him from the wraith of Delta squad on Parinta, Saving Ssophia in the underground river, saving Charlie squad from a Graken attack, and helping the other squads during the survival tournament which ended with him getting injured badly. He continued with how he kept them calm when the Abolefacio was destroyed and finally how he figured out the unwinnable battle that had stumped the Alliance Military Academy students for a long time.

Rostrik looked at Mouse, "Captain Matthews sounds like a great man." Mouse looked up and thought for a moment, "You know you are one hundred percent right, he is and I am grateful I am one of his friends."

Mouse looked over at Rostrik, "What made you want to know what I thought about Caalin?" Rostrik replied, "I had heard a lot of rumors about him being so great, so I decided I would ask someone that has known him longer than all the other people onboard." Mouse smiled, "Well we are great friends but Ssam, Ssophia are just as close and Ang is even closer. We have been through a lot together and I am very grateful to have them all on my side." Rostrik then thanked Mouse for being so open and honest with him, he now had a better appreciation for the Captain.

Mouse looked over to Rostrik, "OK enough about Caalin tell me about you and Faelara and your home planet, I want to know how you wound up as part of our crew." Rostrik thought for a moment, "Well you know Faelara and I are from two different clans even though we are from the same planet. We were basically from two different villages, but our stories are about the same. I will start by telling you about our planet and the customs."

He cleared his throat, "Vireria is made up of large forest, Mountains and larger lakes, and our villages are scattered all over the planet in the forest. We lived off the land and what the forest and lakes provided for us, but that was until the pirates attacked the planet. I was away with a hunting party when my village was attacked and totally destroyed; there were no survivor except from myself and the other four men in the hunting party. The pirates then moved on and attacked Faelara's village but the Alliance ships arrived in time to save the village from the same fate as mine. The pirates did destroy a lot of homes before the

Alliance's arrival, and Faelara's home was one of those destroyed leaving her as the only family member to survive. Her older brother and parents were killed and she was critically injured in the attack and spent three weeks in an Alliance hospital before recovering from her injuries. That is where I met her and together we decided to join the Alliance and do what we could to bring the pirates to justice."

He continued, "We went through Alliance training for security and after that we were assigned to security details on one of the Alliance outpost, but we always wanted to be on a ship, out in space where all the action was. We heard through our chain of command that there was a new ship being commission and turned over to an outstanding but young captain who had accomplished a feat that none of the Alliance Military Academy Students had ever been able to do, he had won the unwinnable battle by thinking outside the box. Even though we did not know anything about the Captain both Faelara and I jumped at the opportunity to join the crew, and thanks to the information you have given me it looks like we made the right decision in joining you. I am sure Faelara will feel the same way once I tell her about everything you have told me."

Mouse smile, "I am glad you feel that way, but don't just take my word about everything, feel free to talk to any of the others about Caalin, I mean Captain Matthews, and you will find that everyone will give you the same information about him. You will also find out that he put other's safety ahead of his own, which tends to get him in trouble with Ang, or I should say Medical Officer Angiliana Avora and Medical Office Ssophia Ssallazz. You see Angiliana happens to be his girlfriend and Ssophia is her best friend, we were all members of the same squad back at Boldoron Academy. Captain Anderson was our medical instructor back then and the Security Advisor Marjori Kai was our Self-Defense instructor and because of Captain Matthews they both volunteered to join the ship's crew."

Rostrik stood up and stretch out his hand to shake Mouse's hand, "I have to make my rounds before I call it a night, but I want to thank you for taking the time to tell me about our Captain. I can tell that he is appreciated by everyone around him." Mouse smiled at Rostrik, "I have to go too, I need to check on the progress of the androids I have working in the shuttle bay then get some rest myself, but if you have any more questions or need any help with anything feel free to come see me, I am always available for friends."

Rostrik then turned and left the dining hall with a smile on his face after hearing that Mouse considered him a friend. After Rostrik had left Mouse got up took his tray over to the dish return area and made his way out of the dining hall and back down to check on his androids. Once Mouse had reached the shuttle bay he checked the androids progress and looked over a few of the drones they had completed. Everything seemed to be going as he had hoped so he decided to call it a night and made his way to his room to get some needed rest.

# CHAPTER 4

||||||||||||||||||||||||||||||||||||||||||

# ACCIDENT IN THE ARMORY

The next morning Mouse was up early and back down in the shuttle bay checking on the androids progress again. He was surprised that everything was almost complete and from his checks all the drones looked to be in working order. As he was going over everything Faelara paused to say good morning to him, she was on her way to the armory to have her team get some weapons ready for the next trip down to Corincas. Mouse told her good morning and let her know that everything on his end had gone as plan so they were all set for the next trip down to the planet. Faelara replied, "That sounds great, so I will see you at the next briefing." She then made her way to the armory to complete her task.

When she arrived at the armory Resrassira was already there pulling some of the weapons that were going to be taken with the team going down to the planet. Faelara asked, "Is that all the weapons are do we need any more?" Resrassira replied, "I think we need one more out of the large box in the corner." Faelara walked over and open the box then pull out one of the laser rifles from inside. She handed the rifle to Resrassira and turned to close the metal box when the lid slammed shut cutting Faelara's arm as it fell. Mouse hearing Faelara scream in pain came running over and seeing how bad she was bleeding, he quickly grabbed a first aid kit from the nearby wall. Resrassira quickly put a tourniquet on Faelara's arm to slow the bleeding while mouse put a makeshift bandage on it. Once they had the blood slowed down they rushed her to the Medical Facility.

As the three of them entered the Medical Facility Ang and Ssophia were going over some paperwork preparing for ship physicals. Mouse shouted to the two of them, "Faelara has a large cut on her arm that needs your attention." The two of them came running over and led Faelara over to an examination table. Ang injected Faelara with some medical nanobots and a sedative to ease the pain, she then turned to Mouse and Resrassira, "She is going to be ok, and the two of you probably have some work to do." Mouse spoke up, "You're right; she is in good hands so we will be off to finish our work." As they were leaving Mouse looked at Resrassira, "They will take good care of Faelara, you probably need to finish up in the armory and I will let Clair know what happened." Resrassira nodded her head, "Thank you for your help, I will get back to my work now." With that complete the two of them left the medical facility and went in separate directions.

Ang had removed the tourniquet and bandage from Faelara's arm and sprayed it with a bio-spray to kill any germs that may have gotten into the wound. Faelara set there staring at the cut as it slowly closed up from the work of the nanobots in her system. Ssophia smiled at her, "Don't worry there won't be a scare the nanobots do a great job at repairing the tissue." Faelara laughed, "I was not worried about a scare I was just amazed with how fast they work." Ang Jumped in, "Well we got use to how fast they work from watching them work on Captain Matthews, while we were in school, he seemed to spend a lot of time getting nanobots injections for one thing or another."

Faelara thought for a moment, "That is right; most of the crew were your classmates, so you all know each other very well." Ssophia smiled, "Well Ang knows Captain Matthews really well, and that is because she is his girlfriend." Ang gave Ssophia a stern look, "Well the same could be said about you and Gahe." Faelara thought for a moment then turned to Ang, "Let me get this right, you and Captain Matthews are in a relationship and Ssophia and Lieutenant Gluskap in Engineering are in one as well?" Sisten had walked in during the conversation and spoke, "Oh and don't forget Morty and I are as well, or should I have said Engineering Office Valtor." Ssophia jumped back in, "Oh and let's not forget that your security officer Clair Tilone and my brother are a couple."

Faelara's brain was spinning from all the information she had just heard so she paused for a moment to get her thoughts together. She looked over to the three girls, "And this involvement with each other does not get in the way of your work?" Ang looked over at Ssophia and Sisten then back to Faelara, "No, it doesn't, we prioritize our work and our relationship has to come after work. Now if you are asking do we worry about the boys when they are on a mission, then the answer is yes, but we would worry about everyone that was on the mission as well." She continued, "It is nice to have someone to come back to and share your thoughts and worries with knowing they are not going to be judgmental." Ssophia put her hand on Faelara's shoulder, "You will find out that every one of our classmates that are now members of the crew are involved with one of the others, and that is why we are all that close."

Faelara then asked, "Doesn't that make it hard to follow orders from Captain Matthews?" Ang answered, "Not at all, we all found out while in school together that Caalin is the best leader we could have, he would not give an order that would endanger anyone unless that was the only thing he could do. He is the type of person who would put himself in harm's way before putting anyone else in danger." Ssophia spoke up, "And he has done that more than he should have, he has saved many lives in the past few years including mine and I cannot think of someone I would rather serve under than Captain Caalin Matthews." Sisten jumped in, "Caalin would rather something happen to him than to anyone else, he was injured badly during our survival tournament our first year at Boldoron but still saved Atira and me after the three of us were buried under some rocks." She continued, "So if you are asking if I would follow Captain Matthews's orders without hesitation."

Ang could see Faelara trying to pull all the information together, "Now with that all said you are wondering if we would follow his orders blindly and the answer is no, if we have worries or doubts we will bring them up, Caalin would not have it any other way. If you think there is something wrong with an order he would expect you to voice your opinion, he would be the first to tell you he is not perfect and can make mistakes." Faelara smile, "Thank you three for being open with me, I now have a better understanding of the Captain."

About that time Clair walked into the Medical Facility and asked, "Faelara are you ok?" Faelara smiled, "Lieutenant Tilone you did not have to come down to check on me." Clair smiled, "You think I would not want to know how one of my friends was doing after what happened." Faelara looked puzzled and Clair put her hand on Faelara's, "You will find out that we all are friends here, and we all watch out for each other, so yes I am going to come down to check on my friend." She then gave Faelara a stern look, "I know I may be a lieutenant in the eyes of the Alliance but I am Clair to my friends and while we are onboard this ship and no Alliance big wigs are around I expect you to call me by my name." Faelara smiled, "Yes Clair I understand." Clair continued,

"And that came straight from Caalin, while onboard this ship we are all a family and family doesn't use ranks."

Clair then stated, "We have a briefing at 15:00 about the next trip back down to Corincas so you need to get some rest I will see you then." Before Clair left she turned to Ang, "Ang, Caalin would like to know if you would have lunch with him at 12:00?" Ang smile, "Please let him know I would be happy too and will meet him in the dining room at that time." Clair smiled, "I will let him know and I will see everyone at the briefing." She then turned and left the room heading back to the bridge. Ang turned to Faelara, "Well you heard Clair, you can rest here or you can go back to your room to get some rest, but make sure you also get something to eat before the briefing this afternoon." Faelara decided to rest in her room and told Ang she would see her at the briefing, and she then stood up and made her way out. Once she reached her room she went straight in and lay down on her bed recounting all the information that she had hear about Captain Matthews. As she lay there she thought to herself, *"I could not have asked to be assigned with a better crew than the crew of the Seeker."*

# CHAPTER 5

||||||||||||||||||||||||||||||||||||||||||||

# LUNCH AND A BRIEFING

Ang made her way to the dining hall to meet Caalin for lunch, as she entered the dining room she could see him sitting at a table on the far side of the room. Caalin stood up as she approached the table, "I am glad you had the time to join me, it has been a while since we enjoyed a meal together." Ang smiled, "You know I will make the time to enjoy a meal with you if it was nothing but a cup of tea." As they took their seats Xaera appeared at their table, "Captain Matthews what could I get for you and Lieutenant Avora?" Caalin looked up at her, "First you can just call us by our first names, everyone onboard this ship is like family to us." Xaera was a little taken back for a moment the nodded her head, "I will do that Caalin and Angiliana." Ang quickly corrected her, "That would just be Ang for me, that is what all my friends call me and we are friends aren't we?" Xaera smiled, "Yes Ang, we are friends."

Caalin then turned to her, "What is the special for today?" Xaera replied,"Zerion stew with a cenato salad." Caalin then turned to Ang, "How does that sound to you?" Ang replied, "That sounds wonderful." Xaera smiled, "I will have them out in a few moments, and I will bring you some of our best tea along with it." Caalin thanked her as she turned and made her way back to the kitchen to get their meals.

Caalin then placed his hand on Ang's and asked, "How is Faelara doing I heard she was injured this morning." Ang replied, "She had a nasty cut on her arm but we took care of it and she went to her room to get a little rest before the briefing this afternoon." Caalin sighed, "That is good to hear it always bothers me when one of my friends gets injured. Why don't we send some food to her room just in case she doesn't have time to eat before the briefing?" Ang smile, "That would be a great idea I will tell Xaera when she returns with our meals."

Xaera returned bringing their food and tea and as she was setting it on the table Ang informed her that they wanted to send some food to Faelara's room. She told her about Faelara's injury and they wanted to make sure she was ok for the upcoming briefing later. Xaera thought for a moment, "I know exactly what to send her, it is one of her favorites, and she will be happy it is coming from you Ang." Ang smiled, "That is great but it was Caalin's idea to send the food." Xaera replied, "That will make her even happier with it coming from the Captain of the ship." She turned and went to prepare the food to take to Faelara.

Caalin was just mentioning to Ang on how hard it was to get time to spend with her when Marty walked up, "Caalin can I talk to you about getting two of the androids once Mouse is done with them, I want to use them to help with the maintenance of the shuttles and to help in the cargo area when needed," Caalin thought for a moment, "I don't see any problem with that at all, I will discuss it with Mouse and the two of you can work out programming them for what is needed."

Jason had walked into the dining hall and over heard the conversation, "Well if you are planning to use the androids in other areas, why don't we designate some for laundry service and cleaning services around the ship" The next thing Caalin and Ang noticed was the crowd around them discussing the use of the androids to help all around the ship. At that moment a voice was heard, "Don't you all know that Caalin and Ang are trying to have a nice lunch and you are bombarding him with things that can be discussed later at our briefing?" Ssophia had walked in and notice the crowd and quickly put a stop to the madness. The group quickly apologized to Ang and Caalin and went on their way. Caalin thanked her for the assistance and invited her to join them. Ssophia shook her head, "You two need a little time together without being bothered; besides Gahe is waiting for me to join him." She then pointed to a table over in another corned and Gahe gave them a wave as they looked his way. Ssophia smiled at the two of them, "Enjoy the rest of your meal; I will see you at the briefing."

Caalin looked over at Ang, "I am sorry for all the commotion, maybe next time we can just have a private diner in my cabin." Ang placed her hand on top of his, "That would be nice; there would not be any interruption there." After lunch Caalin informed Ang he had to get back to the bridge and he would see her later at the briefing then left her smiling as he walked off. As Ang was leaving to head back to the Medical facility Ssophia joined her and the two of them walked back down together.

Later that afternoon at the briefing Caalin welcomed everyone and thanked them for attending, he then turned to Mouse, "Do you have all the drones ready to go?" Mouse replied, "I do but there are so many they will not fit in the shuttle we used last time, we will need to take a larger shuttle down this time." Caalin thought for a moment, "No I think we should take two shuttles. It would be a lot faster if we sent one shuttle to the northern hemisphere and one to the southern hemisphere, that would allow use to complete the survey quicker so we could move on to the other two planets." Mouse replied, "That would, I will have to make a minor change to their program so they cover their designated areas but that should only take about an hour to do." Caalin smiled, "That is great, we will use two shuttles then, once you have them programmed load half on AS1-S1 and the others on AS1-S2 we will use those shuttles for the mission."

Caalin then turned his attention to who would be going on the mission and announced, "Ok for this mission AS1-S1 will consist of Ang, Ssam, Mouse, Rostrik and I, while AS1-S2 will have Jason, Gahe, Ssophia and Resrassira." He continued, "Mouse work with Gahe so he know everything he needs to about the drones, Ssophia you will be in charge of concealing the shuttle on the way down and act as medical backup should anyone get injured." Ssophia smiled, "You can count on me; I can handle both tasks." Caalin then turned to Rostrik and Resrassira, "The two of you are in charge of security, make sure everyone gets back safely." Rostrik looked over at Resrassira then back to Caalin, "You can count on us Caalin."

Caalin smiled, "With that we have our teams; we will depart at 06:00 in the morning, Marty when Mouse and Gahe complete the reprogramming of the drone please make sure that they are loaded on the shuttles for us." Marty nodded his head, "Consider it done Caalin." Before he dismissed everyone he turned to Mouse again, "Oh and Mouse since you are done with all the androids I would like you to program them to do some other jobs on the ship. If you will get with Jason and Marty I think they have a few jobs they would like some help with." Mouse laughed, "I was thinking the same thing, and I will get with them after I am done with the drones." Caalin smiled, "Great, since we have our teams for tomorrow everyone is dismissed, I will see you at 06:00 in the shuttle bay."

As Caalin and Dargon were leaving the conference room he leaned over to Dargon, "I am sorry for leaving you to handle the ship while I go on the away mission, but I promise you that you can handle the next one." Dargon patted him on the shoulder, "I know you want to see that things are working properly before turning it over to me so I am ok with it." Caalin replied, "Great I could not leave the safety of the Seeker in better hands."

# CHAPTER 6

||||||||||||||||||||||||||||||||||||||||||||

# SECOND SURVEY MISSION

The next morning Caalin was up at 03:00 and made his way to the bridge, Ric had just taken over navigation from Evalon when Caalin entered. Caalin spoke, "Good morning Ric, how are things looking?" Ric replied, "I just got here myself and relived Evalon, but I was just about to do a scan of the asteroid field." He then turn and pushed a few buttons and watched his monitor, "Looks like everything is clear for your mission, there are a few asteroids close but they are drifting away from our area." Caalin smiled, "That is great news." Astra turned around from her seat, "The communications lines have been clear all night with no messages from Alliance Headquarters." Caalin quickly apologized for not saying good morning to her, he had just not seen her setting there. She smiled at him, "These seat backs are pretty high and you had other things on your mind so there is no need to apologize."

Asgaya came in and seeing Caalin at the Captains chair, "Well good morning Caalin, I see this is where you are, Ang was looking for you, she said she had stopped by your room but no one answered. She was heading toward the dining hall to see if you are having breakfast." Caalin jumped from his seat, "Thanks for the information, I think I will head there now to join her." He then told everyone to carry on with their duties Dargon would be there later, and then off to the dining hall he went.

When he reached the dining hall Ang was standing there looking around to see if he was at any of the tables, he walked up behind her, "Are you looking for someone?" Ang jumped, "Oh you startled me and yes I was looking for a handsome young man to have breakfast with." Caalin looked around the room, "Well there is Ekdrin and Jhevendahl over there and there is your cousin Aeron but Tealana is with him." Ang turned and looked him right in the eyes, "Ok you know exactly who I was looking for so stop kidding me." Caalin laughed, "I can't help it you are so adorable when you get flustered." There was a voice from behind them, "Caalin is absolutely right about that", it was Ssophia and Gahe was with her. Gahe spoke up, "Mind if we join you for breakfast?" Caalin looked at Ang and she smiled, "We would love to have the two of you join us." The four of them then made their way to a table along the wall and took their seats.

Jhalia quickly came over to find out what they would like for breakfast while she poured them some hot tea. They all placed their orders and sat back sipping the tea while talking about the mission. As their food was coming out Belrion came out to let Caalin know that they had sent meals down to be loaded on the shuttle, Mouse had informed him it may take two days to complete the survey and he wanted them to have something nutritious to eat. Caalin thanked him but he held his hand up as to stop Caalin, "Well to be honest it was Tehaena's idea and she made all the meals herself." Ang jumped into the conversation, "Well give Tehaena our thanks, I know we will enjoy the meals."

Ekdrin and Jhevendahl were on their way out but stopped by Caalin's table to let him know that the shuttles had been loaded and were ready whenever they were. Caalin thanked them for the information and then turn back to finish his meal. While they were eating the rest of the two shuttle teams had entered and were enjoying their breakfast. Jason stopped by and asked Caalin, "Before we depart can we look at the map of Corincas and decide the best areas to land and deploy the drones from?" Caalin thought for a moment, "That sounds like a great idea; we want the best location to get full coverage of the planet. We can use the computer system in the cargo bay to check out the planet."

Caalin finished his breakfast then excused himself telling Ang and the others he would see them in the shuttle bay later, he needed to go to the bridge to check on some things. Ang smiled at him, "Go already you don't have to explain everything to us, you are the captain of this ship and have things you have to do." He smiled at her, "See you in a few then turned and left the room.

When Caalin reached the bridge Dargon was there looking over the reports from the night shift. He looked up from the tablet he had in his hand, "What are you doing here; I thought you would be enjoying breakfast about this time." Caalin replied, "I just had breakfast but I need to bring up the map we have of Corincas I want to see what good landing area we can find to release the drones and stay out of sight." Dargon brought up the map of the planet on one of the large screens the walked over to join Caalin to help look. Caalin told Dargon, "We need locations that are as close to the center of both hemispheres to release the drones; I will watch the northern while you watch the southern. Let me know if you spot anything and we can zoom in to check it out."

As the planet map slowly moved in from of them Caalin's eyes were fixed on the northern hemisphere until he saw something that caught his eyes and he stopped the map. There was a small valley filled with trees right in front of him. He zoomed in closer and found a small clearing just large enough to land the shuttle then move it under the trees. He pinned the spot and restarted the mapped, but as soon as he did Dargon stopped it again and pointed to a location on the southern hemisphere that was mountainous with a lot of large caves. They zoomed in on the location and found a cave large enough to land the shuttle in, so they pinned that location. They looked and looked until they had four different locations on the map pinned as possible landing spots. Caalin thanked Dargon for the help and made his way out and down to the shuttle bay.

When Caalin got to the shuttle bay he had everyone follow him to the cargo bay area and brought up one of the computers. He showed everyone the four different landing possibilities, two in each hemisphere then he let Jason know to start with the first one and if it was not a suitable landing spot then move on to the next one. One of the two locations should work but he was leaving it up to Jason to make the decision, but to remember they needed to be able to stay undetected.

As everyone was boarding their designated shuttle Caalin told them to stay safe and watch out for each other. He then told Jason, "Send us a quick but short message once your team has completed then make your way back to the Seeker, we will do the same." Jason replied, "We will, but you keep your team safe." Everyone boarded the shuttles and they lifted off and exited the ship slowly making their way out of the asteroid field. Once they had cleared the field Ssam made AS1-S1 disappear and Ssophia made AS1-S2 do the same. Both shuttles moved in two different directions as they made their way to their designated landing areas.

Twenty minutes after they had left the Seeker AS1-S1 was making its way down to the first landing area and Caalin was bringing it downing into the small clearing he had locate on the map. Once he had the ship near the ground he slowly moved it up under the trees so it could not be seen from above and set it down.

AS1-S2 had also reached the first designated landing areas and as Caalin had thought the cave was not only large enough for the shuttle to land in, but it was large enough for it to turn completely around. Seeing this Jason took it in and turned it to face the entrance just in case they needed to leave quickly then set it down genteelly.

# CHAPTER 7

‖‖‖‖‖‖‖‖‖‖‖‖‖‖‖‖‖‖‖‖‖‖‖‖‖‖‖‖‖‖‖‖‖

# CORINCAS SECOND VISIT

Mouse had calculated that it would take the drones at least thirty six to thirty eight hours to complete the scan of the entire planet so they would be spending the night on the ground. Caalin slowly opened the shuttle door and walked out under the trees to check the area out. He could hear the sounds of the bird like creators as they flew over head and the roar in the distance of some of the creators that were wondering around them. He turned to the others, "Well this looks like a good place to set up camp, Mouse can go ahead and launch the drones."

Ssam and Rostrik assisted Mouse in getting the drones out of the shuttle and out of the crates that the cargo team had put them in for the trip. Once all the drones were on the ground Mouse launched them into the sky. Once they were airborne they began spacing themselves out as they flew north to begin their scan. Mouse turned to Caalin, "It will take them about an hour to reach their starting point then they will turn east and begin their scan. I estimate it will take them at least four trips around the planet to complete the northern hemisphere and that should be the same for Jason's team."

Caalin replied, "That means we should be heading back to the Seeker late tomorrow so we need to setup the security fencing around our area to prevent any wild animal getting to close to the ship." The Moment he has said that Rostrik was walking out of the shuttle carrying some large rods with glass looking balls on them spaced about 30 centimeters apart, "I'm way ahead of you with the fencing." Ssam was right behind him with another load of the rods. They placed the rods ten meters apart circling the shuttle with at least twenty meters between them and the shuttle.

Caalin told the group he was going to fly around and check out the area to see if there was anything they really needed to worry about. Ang walked over to Caalin before he could lift of the ground, "Would it be ok if I accompany you?" Caalin smiled, "That would be fine, I know you want to stretch your wings." Just as soon as they took off Mouse turned to the others, "Why don't we gather some fire wood since we don't know how cool it will get tonight and I don't want to be cooped up in the shuttle the entire time we are here." Ssam and Rostrik agreed and the three of them began collecting fire wood.

Once Caalin and Ang were in the air Ang asked, "Are you planning to fly south to check on the others?" Caalin smiled at her, "You read me like a book, I plan on checking the first location only because I pretty sure that is where they landed, plus it would take too long to check the other one if they decided to move on to it." Ang laughed, "I think the real reason is the first location is the only one that we can get to and get back before dark, am I correct." Caalin glanced in her direction, "Again you read me like a book."

After about three hours of fast flying the two of them finally reached the location that Jason's team should have landed. Caalin scanned the cliff with his eyes until he saw the opening and made his way to it. The two of them landed at the opening of the cave and were quickly greeted by

Resrassira, "Welcome you two; well Ssophia had it right when she said not to be surprised if the two of you showed up here." Ang spoke, "Well Ssophia knows Caalin almost, if not better than I do, but we had talked about it last night and thought he would do this." Caalin turned to her, "Are you two all ways one step ahead of me, I didn't think about doing this until we landed." Ssophia had just walked up laughing, "When it comes to you, you are so easy for us to predict, although there are some of your crazy ideas we can't predict." Ang looked over at Caalin, "Yes and most of those are the ones that get you injured."

Caalin just shook his head in disbelief and walked further into the cave toward the shuttle. Jason and Gahe were sitting at the rear of the shuttle when Caalin walked around. Jason stood up, "Well Ssophia did tell us to expect a visit from you; I guess you are here to see how things are going?" Caalin just smiled, "I just wanted to make sure you guys made it safely and there were no technical issues." Gahe replied, "We launched all the drones without any problems and they all made their way south like they were programmed. Mouse told us it would be around thirty six hours before they return so we are just killing time until then."

Caalin looked around the area and could see the back wall of the cave and had noticed as they were landing how sheer the cliff was outside so nothing could climb up and into the cave. He looked over at Jason, "You have a pretty secure location here we had to put up a security perimeter at ours." Jason replied, "Yeah after I looked around the area I decided we did not need to go that far, but I am planning to set up some light out here for later." Caalin smiled, "You may want to pull out some portable heaters as well; it may get cooler after nightfall." Gahe looked over at Jason, I will start pulling them out now, thanks for the idea Caalin I wouldn't want the girls to get cold."

Ssophia had just walked up and looking in Gahe direction, "Speak for yourself Gahe Gluskap us girls are not as delicate as you think." Gahe jumped, "I'm sorry that is not what I meant." Ssophia laughed, "I know I just wanted to give you a little scare." The group started laughing and Caalin looked over at Ang, "I think we should be heading back, they have everything in control here and Mouse is going to start worrying if we are not back before dark."

As Ang and Caalin were making their way back to the cave entrance he told Jason, "As soon as the drones make it back load them into your shuttle and head back to the Seeker." Jason replied, "We will do that and will see you back on board the ship." Ang took off into the sky and Caalin followed after her flying down low and checking out the bottom of the cliff. During their flight back they notice the bird like creators that looked like small feathered lizard and along the ground were a herd of grazing animals that were large and covered in wooly hair. They flew over a spot where water was shooting up at least twenty meters into the air and forming a river that ran down into a large lake.

They finally came in for a landing at the edge of the tree line and walked back into camp where Mouse had a fire already going and the three guys were sitting around having a meal. Ssam looked up, "Well how is Jason's team doing?" Mouse quickly jumped in, "I hope they didn't have any problems with the drones." Caalin looked at the two of them, "How did you know we went to check on them?" Ssam smile, "Ang told us you would more than like do it, and we were certain of it when we saw you heading south." Caalin just shook his head then turned to Mouse, "All the drones lifted off without a problem. I informed Jason that once they all return to pack them up and head back to the ship, you can pull the data from them when we get back."

While they were talking Ang had made her way into the shuttle and had come out with two meals that Tehaena had her husband Belrion pack for them. She walked over to Caalin and handed one to him, "Here why don't we set down and enjoy a meal before Mouse eats everything." Mouse looked over at Ang, "I am fine thank you, but I did see that Tehaena did pack us one of my favorite deserts so I am heading back inside for that." Ang laughed, "If it is one of her deserts I can't blame you, but you better save some for the rest of us." Rostrik jumped up, "I will make sure he doesn't eat them all, besides I want some myself." The five of them set around the fire laughing and telling stories until it got late.

Caalin quickly set up a roster for watch, he wanted someone awake at all times just in case something happened. They were to not only watching for any intruders but listening for any radio calls from the Seeker or AS1-S2. Since it was only eight hours until daylight Mouse would take the first two hours, then Ssam, Rostrik and Caalin would take the last two before daylight. Ang looked at Caalin, "OK, why am I the only one not standing any watch?" Caalin just looked at her, "We can't have our Medical Officer standing watch, what if there is some type of emergency and we need medical assistance we can have you tired."

The watch went ok during the night and Caalin was now doing his sitting outside near the fire remembering the evenings setting near the fire during the survival tournament. There was a sound from behind him and he quickly turned to see Ang standing there watching him. He asked, "What are you doing up." She smiled at him, "I woke up about five minutes ago and was just standing here watching you." He patted the seat next to him, "Why don't you come join me then." She made her way over and set down next to him, "You were remembering the nights during the survival tournament weren't you?" Caalin looked over at her,

"You have to stop reading my minded it is creeping me out how well you do it." Ang laughed, "I didn't read your mind I was doing the same thing myself. I was remembering the night we experimented with your abilities and figured out you were actually controlling gravity." Caalin laughed, "Yeah and it was fun wakening Ssam up by dropping those little rocks on his head."

Ang thought for a moment, "Do you know what my best memory is of all the memories of our time together?" Caalin thought for a moment, "It would be hard to guess I have so many good memories with you." Ang leaned over and kissed him, "Silly my best memory was when you learned to use you power to fly and we took our first flight together. That was when I realized we would be able to do a lot more things together and you could see everything the same way I could, from above." Caalin reached over and took her hand, "You are right I do love flying with you, there is nothing else like it. I am so grateful to Jo for teaching me how to use my power to fly."

Caalin looked up into the sky, "I wonder what Jo is doing now?" There was a voice from behind them, "Probably having a good time with Nam." Ssam had just came out and overheard Caalin last statement, "Oh I am sorry I did not mean to scare the two of you I just woke up and thought I would get some fresh air." Caalin laughed, "Its ok we were just reminising about the memories we have made together."

Ang looked over to Ssam, "What is your favorite memory from our time together?" Ssam did not have to think long, "It would be finding my grandfather with the help of all my friends, I can't think of anything that is better than that." Ang replied, "Yeah that was a great memory and I am glad we were able to finish Ziggy's mission, but I do miss that old character." Caalin squeezed her hand a little, "We all miss Ziggy;

he was one of a kind and hard to forget." The three of them set outside talking for another hour before Mouse and Rostrik joined them.

As the five of them were eating their breakfast Rostrik asked Ssam how he was able to make the shuttle invisible. Ssam explained that he wasn't making it invisible but was just bending the light around it. He said, "You know how the shield generator puts a shield around the ship to protect it for being hit, I basically do the same thing with light."

Ssam's comment about how he bends light being similar to how the shield generator works set Mouse's brain in to motion and he started thinking about if he could make changes to a shield generator to do the same thing.

After breakfast Ssam and Rostrik went out to do some exploring, while Ang and Caalin went for another flight, and Mouse stayed back to look at some schematics on the shuttles computer. It was later in the afternoon before everyone had gotten back and decided to have a meal since they had all missed lunch. While eating Caalin asked Mouse what time did he think the drones should be returning? Mouse checked the time, "They should be returning within the next couple of hours." Caalin replied, "Great once they are back let's get them on board the shuttle and get back to the Seeker I think I would like a hot shower." Ang jumped in, "I know I would love a hot shower myself."

They all set around for another hour then Caalin helped Rostrik and Ssam take down the security fence and pack it away in the shuttle. A few minutes after they had the fence pack Mouse could see the drones making their way down into the clearing. They moved the storage containers out to the clearing and started collecting and packing the drones for the trip back to the Seeker.

Once everything was secured in the shuttle Caalin using his power picked up the shuttle and moved it out from under the tress back into the clearing. He then made his way to the pilot seat and had everyone take their seats. Slowly they lifted off the ground and up through the sky as Ssam made them invisible. Soon they were entering the asteroid field and nearing the Seeker as they got closer they reappeared and Ssam sent a message to have the shuttle bay opened so they could land. They bay doors opened and Caalin brought the shuttle in and landed it right next to AS1-S2 that had arrive about ten minutes earlier.

The Cargo team was unloading the storage container with the drones from Jason's shuttle as Caalin brought his to a halt. Caalin asked Mouse, "Where do you need the drones?" Mouse replied, "Just leave them in the containers by the shuttles. I can bring them online remotely and pull all the data without having to remove them from the containers. I will also program them for the next mission if you will let me know which planet is next on your list."

Caalin thought for a moment, "OK I think we will survey Kritilia next so program them for that planet." Mouse replied, "I will take care of it and they will be ready in a few hours." Caalin put his hand on Mouse's shoulder, "There is not a rush tomorrow afternoon will be fine, get a shower and some rest, I am going to schedule the next mission for the day after tomorrow." Mouse came back with, "OK but I am going to put all the data from the drones before I leave the shuttle bay, you can view it in a couple of hours." Caalin then told everyone, "Go get a shower and some rest." With that being said everyone made their way out of the shuttle bay area, with the exception of Mouse who stayed back to pull the data.

As Caalin was leaving the shuttle bay he stopped and asked Devlon to let Dargon know he will get with him after he had a chance to shower and changed. Devlon replied, "I will see that he get the message now go get cleaned up, I will see if I can give Mouse any assistance." Caalin thanked him and headed off to his room.

# CHAPTER 8

||||||||||||||||||||||||||||||||||||||||||||||

# BACK FROM THE MISSION

Caalin had gotten cleaned up and made his way to the bridge to talk with Dargon, and once he arrive he ask Dargon to join him in the briefing room. They made their way to the room and took their seats with Caalin bringing up the planet Kritilia as a hologram. He then turned to Dargon, "The next mission you will take the lead, I will select the teams but you are in charge of the mission itself." Dargon looked at him, "Who do you have in mind for the mission." Caalin answered, "Well besides yourself on AS1-S1 you will have Ssam, Mouse, Sisten and Faelara. Clair will be in charge of AS1-S2 with her crew of Ssophia, Gahe, Resrassira and I think Marjori Kai should go along to give her some experience off the ship." Dargon looked perplexed, "Why do you want to send Kai on this one?" Caalin just smiled, "She has been on board since I took command of this ship and I know she has not had enough to keep her busy so I want to give her a break from the boredom." Dargon thought for a moment then agree that was a good idea.

Caalin then pointed to the map of Kritilia, "Now we need to pick some locations that look like good landing spots for your mission." The two of them stared at the map until they found four good landing locations, two in the north and two in the south." Caalin patted Dargon on the shoulder, "With that done I leave it to you to decide who takes the north and south locations. Oh and you will be giving the briefing, I am scheduling it for tomorrow after lunch and your teams can leave the next morning." Dargon turn to join Caalin on the way out, "That sounds good to me, by the way when are we going to have the data from your mission."

Mouse had just arrived on the bridge and over heard the comment, "I have the data available right now." He handed Caalin a tablet and informed him, "There is no other life forms on the planet except for the animals that inhabit it and there is no pirate basic down there either." Caalin turned to Dargon, "With one planet cleared you need to be extra cautious on your mission, I want everyone back here safe." Dargon looked Caalin in the eyes, "I want everyone back safe as well so we will be on our toes while we are down there." Caalin then looked around the bridge and told Dargon, "I think our location is secure enough that with the sensor array we have running we can scale our watch down a lot. There is no reason one person could not handle the bridge during our down time." Dargon agreed with him and stated he would change the roster around to reflect the change.

Caalin then said, "I am going to get something to eat then I will man the bridge until 22:00 so change your roster allow the crew some time for themselves." Dargon laughed, "Now how did I know you were going to say something like that." Caalin came back with, "Now don't you start reading my mind like Ang and Ssophia does." Dargon and Mouse both laughed with Mouse saying, "It's because you are so predictable." Caalin just shook his head as he walked out heading for the dining hall. Mouse left and made his way back down to engineering and once there he set down at one of the computers in the room to do some research.

He pulled up a several schematics and started looking at the parts he could change to make a shield generator into a stealth generator. He finally came up with a plan for a refractor generator but needed the perfect crystal to put in it to make it work. He set there going through an array of different crystal to see if they would work and finally found one, it was an azerithium crystal which he did not have nor knew where to get one. He saved his new schematic and then went to his room to get cleaned up and go to the dining hall since he was now getting hungry. He decided after dinner he would go back to his quarters and use his computer to do a search for where to find an azerithium crystal and see what it looked like.

The next morning after breakfast Mouse went back down to the shuttle bay where the containers with the drones set next to the shuttles. Marion and Jhenestin walked over and asked if he was ready for the drones to be put back on board the shuttles. Mouse asked them to give him about a half an hour to reprogram them and then they could reload them. Marion nodded, "We will be back in a half an hour to check on you and to load them." Mouse took his tablet out and began his program that reprogrammed all the drones for Kritilia, since it was a little larger than Corincas he set them to fly a little faster to complete the mission in around the same amount of time as it took on the first mission. Once it was completed he let Mar know he was done and they could load the drones back on board the shuttles.

As Mar and Jhenestin were loading the drones Nasth from the kitchen came down to talk to them, he wanted to know what time he should have the meals for the mission down to be loaded for the next mission. Mar Looked over at Jhenestin, "J do you think if they get the meals down here by 04:00 that would be plenty of time to get them stored away for the next group?" Jhenestin nodded his head, "That would give us plenty of time to store them on board." Nasth smile, "Great we will have them here at 04:00."

The next morning at 10:00 Dargon arrived on the bridge to find Caalin already there, "Now you did not stay on the bridge all night did you?" Caalin laughed, "No, I just woke up early and decided to come up and use Mouse's data from the Corincas survey to update the map of the planet." Dargon sighed, "That's good because if Ang heard you had we both would have been in trouble, you for doing it and me for letting you." Just then there was a voice from behind Dargon, "Letting who do what?" Dargon jumped, "Well I came in and found Caalin already here and was just wondering had he been here all night." Ang gave Caalin a stern look, "Well were you here all night?" Caalin broke out in laughter, "No I just got here before Dargon and was updating the map of Corincas with our new data." Ang smiled, "Well I can let the two of you off this time, but I better not catch you pulling an all-nighter on the bridge without a good reason."

She paused for a moment, "Well Captain Matthews would you care to join me for an early lunch, I have a couple of physical scheduled afterwards." Caalin smiled at her as he handed Dargon his tablet, "I would love to, I will be back in a little while Dargon." Dargon chuckled, "Take your time; the bridge isn't going anywhere, at least not without the rest of the ship." Caalin and Ang laughed as they left heading to the dining hall.

When they arrived in the dining hall Jean and Marjori were there having lunch, Jean spotted the two of them and flagged them over. She looked at Caalin, "Why don't the two of you join us we haven't had a chance to talk since we left Gama-12." Before Caalin could say a word Ang spoke up, "We would love too." The four of them set talking with

Jean about all the equipment she had been checking and the notes she had for upgrades when they finally get back to Alliance Headquarters. Marjori thanked Caalin for putting her on the second mission team because she was getting bored not having much to do while on board. Caalin told her, "Maybe we can take one of the larger storage rooms not in use right now and convert it into a training room and you can help keep everyone up on their hand to hand combat skills." Marjori smiled, "That would be great we can't have everyone getting rusty."

Jean and Marjori said they needed to go get some work done and they would see Caalin at the briefing later. Once they were gone Ang looked over at Caalin, "Thank you for coming up with something for Marjori to do I could tell she was getting a little depressed not being able to help in any way." Caalin told Ang, "It is my fault I should have thought of this earlier, I was just concentrating on our mission to much and not my crew, but I will have her training room ready along with a bunch of trainees by the time she gets back from the mission." Ang gave Caalin a quick kiss on the cheek, "You're the best, but I have to run I have some physicals to do, I will talk to you later."

When Caalin returned to the bridge Mouse was there talking with Dargon. Dargon looked over to Caalin, "Have you ever heard of an azerithium crystal?" Caalin looked puzzled, "No why?" Mouse quickly jumped in, "I think I can build a generator that we can connect to the shield generator to bend light around the Seeker the same way Ssam and Ssophia does." Caalin still puzzled, "What does that have to do with an azerithium crystal?" Dargon replied, "It seems that crystal is a key component he needs to build this generator."

Caalin took his seat and thought for a moment, "Well if Mouse says he can build it then I think it's worth a shot, but I know nothing about this azerithium crystal he needs for it." He looked up at the two of them, "We will have to wait until we finish our mission here in the Eridani Nebula and make our way back to Alliance space before I can see what they know about your crystal, so your plan will have to wait until then." Mouse had a disappointed look on his face, "Yeah I know you're right, it would be too dangerous to contact them without knowing if there are pirates around or not."

The three of them moved to the briefing room and Mouse brought up his schematic and was telling them about it when it came time for the mission briefing for the Kritilia mission. Everyone started showing up and the room began to fill. Once everyone had their seats Caalin turned it over to Dargon and he began going over the list for the away teams and which shuttle they were assigned, he also reminded them that they would be leaving at 06:00. Clair let them know she would make sure everyone on her team would make it back safely.

Dargon reminded her that once their drones returned to the shuttle they were to pack them up and head straight back to the ship, his team would do the same. Before the meet was over he went over the landing areas that he and Caalin had picked out, "Remember if the first site is not suitable move to the second one." Mouse stood up, "I have recalibrated all the drones and even thought Kritilia is a little larger than Corincas they should finish the survey in the same amount of time. We should not be on the ground no longer than thirty six to thirty eight hours."

After the briefing everyone left to prepare for the mission and Caalin went back to the bridge, after about an hour he made his was down to the medical facility to see Ang. As he walked in Ang looked up from the computer she was setting at, "Oh hi, what brings our wonderful captain down to see us; you're not feeling ill are you?" Caalin smiled, "No the moment I saw your beautiful face I started feeling great." A voice from behind Caalin spoke, "Oh will you two stop with the mushy stuff." It was Ssophia and Sisten, Ssophia had made the comment and all Sisten could do is giggle at it.

The two girls walked off toward the other side of the facility and Caalin leaned over and whispered, "Meet me in the briefing room at 18:00." Ang looked at him with a smile, "Why would you want me to do that?" Caalin just leaned in and gave her a quick kiss, "It's a secret so I will see you then." He then turned and walked out of the room leaving her a little red. Ssophia walked over and asked, "What did lover boy need?" Ang smiled, "I think he just asked me to have dinner alone with him." Ssophia smiled, "Well it is nice to see he is starting to come around, he might make a good boyfriend after all." The two of them broke into laughter and Ang looked back down at the computer to finish her work.

Later Caalin was in the briefing room with Orianna and Maeria, from the kitchen, setting up a table for a nice quite dinner with Ang. Once they had finish the two girls were on their way out when Ang arrive with her hands behind her back, "Well again it looks like I was right." Caalin looked a little be surprised, "Right about what?" She then brought her hands from behind her back holding a bottle of germanium cider and two glasses, "That you had invited me to a dinner for two." Caalin just lowered his head, "Well I must be easy to read, it seems everyone is doing it lately." Ang just laughed, "It is only because we all know you so well and we know how you treat everyone like family, and that is why I fell in love with you." Caalin smiled and pulled her chair out for her to take a seat, "Well have a seat my lovely girlfriend." Ang took her seat, "Thank you my wonderful boyfriend." The two of them set sipping the cider and enjoying the meal and each other's company completely

46

uninterrupted by anyone, which was the first time since they boarded the ship.

After dinner Caalin walked her back to her cabin only stopping at the dining hall to let Orianna and Maeria that they were done and to thank them for all their help. The two girls told him it was no problem they were happy to do it and anytime that he and Ang needed some time together they would be happy to help. Ang smiled and thanked them as well then her and Caalin made their way down to her cabin. Caalin kissed her goodnight, "Tonight was the best night I have had since we came onboard; I hope we get a chance to do this again." Ang smiled at him, "Any time you want to I am ready, and I had a wonderful time too." Caalin made his way back to his cabin and went straight to bed; he wanted to be in the shuttle bay before Dragon's teams left for their mission.

# CHAPTER 9

⁓⁓⁓⁓⁓⁓⁓⁓⁓⁓⁓⁓⁓⁓⁓⁓⁓⁓⁓⁓⁓⁓⁓⁓⁓⁓⁓

# SURVEY OF KRITILIA

The next morning Caalin arrived in the shuttle bay at 04:30, he wanted to be there when Dargon's teams left to make their way down to Kritilia. Once he arrived he noticed Mar and Jhenestin loading the food containers on the shuttles so he walked over and began helping them. Jhenestin looked over at him, "Captain you don't have to do that we can take care of all this ourselves." Caalin smiled, "Nonsense, I am here and if I can help my crew I will." Mar turned to Jhenestin, "Don't worry J that is just the way Caalin is; he tends to go out of his way to help others." Caalin laughed, "Oh and please remember to call me Caalin, no need to call me Captain unless we are around dignitaries."

They had just loaded the last of the containers when Dargon and his teams arrived. Dargon walked over to Caalin, "I figured you would show up before we left but didn't think you would beat us here and be loading our shuttles for us." Caalin chuckled, "Well I did come down to see you all off, and since I was here I thought it would be good to help my crew members with their work." Dargon asked, "Would you like to say anything to the teams before we leave?" Caalin replied, "Not really, but before I came down I checked the long range scanner for Kritilia and it looks like the northern hemisphere has a few snow storms going

48

on so be prepared and stay safe." Dargon smiled at Caalin, "Thanks for the weather report we will do our best and everyone will get back safely."

The teams loaded the shuttles and they lifted off making their way out of the ship and through the asteroid field. As the two shuttles exited the asteroid field Ssam and Ssophia made them disappear from view and the shuttles were on their way to Kritilia. A few minutes later they were approaching the planet and the two shuttles separated with Clair's team heading south and Dargon's heading north. After a while Dargon's team can to a valley area with the first location that he and Caalin had picked out. There was a large over hang that would shield the shuttle from being detected from above so Dargon brought the shuttle down and slowly maneuvered in under the overhang. Once on the ground Dargon, Mouse and Ssam started pulling the drone's storage container off the shuttle and placing the drone on the ground. Faelara and Sisten pull out the security fence rods out and started placing them around the area to secure their base of operation.

After thirty minutes the security fence was up and working and Mouse was getting ready to launch the drones. Once everyone was back at the shuttle the drones were launched and began spacing their selves out as they move north toward the polar area to begin their survey. Mouse then turned to the others, "Well we have a long boring thirty six hours to wait for them all to return so let's all get comfortable." Ssam and Faelara had already started looking for some fire wood to build a warm fire they could sit around.

At the southern hemisphere Clair and her team found a large wooded area to land in and squeeze up under some trees. Gahe and Ssophia immediately started unloading the drones and Resrassira and Marjori began setting up the perimeter fencing to keep unwanted creators out. Clair began helping Ssophia and Gahe with the drones and it wasn't long before they had them airborne and on their way. Resrassira and Marjori finished the security fence and came back to join the others. Gahe smile, "I think I will gather some wood and build us a fire to stay warm tonight and give us a little more light." Ssophia looked around at the area, "I will come help I think we might need a lot of fire wood."

Both teams had collected fire wood, built fires, had lunch then collected more fire wood and as it slowly got dark they all built up their fires bigger before setting down for dinner. In the north Dargon's team was now experiencing snow fall, it was light at first but began to get heavier as it got later. Dargon told everyone, "We need to move back inside the shuttle, the snow is starting to get deeper and I don't need anyone getting sick from being out in it." Ssam dosed the fire and they all moved inside and close the hatch. Mouse smiled, "Well it looks like we should just settle in for the night and try to get some sleep we can see how deep it gets in the morning." Everyone made their selves comfortable and tried to get some sleep.

In the south Resrassira told everyone she thought they were being watched, she could not see anyone but she could feel them out there. Marjori asked, "Do you know where they are?" Resrassira replied, "About five meters outside our fence due south of us." Marjori then whispered to them, "Why don't you and Ssophia move inside, then Ssophia you make the two of you invisible, you can then come back out and move west outside the fence and see if you can come up behind them." She then turned to Resrassira, "Don't forget to take weapons with you, but only use them if you need to and only on stun, we don't want to hurt anyone if we can avoid it."

The two girls went inside the shuttle out of everyone sight, then Ssophia made them invisible and they came back out and moved west toward the fence. Once they were at the fence Resrassira deactivated one small section and they walked through and she reactivated it. Slowly they made their way south and could hear rustling in the bushes and as they got closer they saw two small children, both girls, staring toward the shuttle. Ssophia spoke, "Can we help the two of you?" the kids turn to look and see who had come up behind them but Ssophia and Resrassira was still invisible." One of the little girls screamed and the other one asked, "Are you a ghost" Ssophia and Resrassira reappeared and Ssophia said, "I am sorry I did not mean to scare the two of you, no we are not ghosts, but what are the two of you doing in this forest alone?"

The two little girls finally calmed down and the one who had spoke earlier replied, "We were out looking for herbs and berries today and got lost, we saw your fire and thought maybe we could ask for some food, but we did not know what that large thing is you are setting by." Ssophia smiled at the girls, "Why don't the two of you come with us and we will get you something to eat and tell you all about our shuttle." The two girls were still scared but they were so hungry they had no choice but to go with them. On the way back to the shuttle Ssophia asked what their names were and found out the blue haired one was Dannona and the green haired one was Tinne. Resrassira deactivated the fence and they reentered the secure area, reactivating it once they had passed through, and walked up to the shuttle.

As the four of them reached the shuttle Clair asked, "Well who are these two lovely little ladies?" Ssophia spoke up, "Let me introduce Ms Dannona and Ms Tinne, it seems the two of them got lost and have not had anything to eat all day." Gahe jumped up, "Well we cannot have these young ladies starving on us; I will get them something to eat right now." He went inside the shuttle and soon returned with plenty of food to feed the two hungry girls.

As the girls were eating Marjori said, "Well it is too late for us to try and get these two home tonight, but first thing in the morning we need to try and locate their village and get them back to their parents, I am sure they are worried about them." She then bent down to the girls, "You two will stay with us tonight and we will help get you home tomorrow is that ok with the two of you?" The two girls looked at each other then nodded their heads yes and continued to eat. After the girls had finished eating Clair got them settles in inside the shuttle to get some sleep, while Gahe set a place up outside for his self and settled down.

Ssophia walked out and set down next to him, "It has been one heck of a night, I'm sorry they took you birth in the shuttle." Gahe smiled over at Ssophia, "It is ok; I know you are worried about those two little ones so I am happy to let them have my bed." Ssophia leaned over and kissed him, "That is why I love you." She then made her way back inside telling him good night as she left."

The next morning Gahe had breakfast ready when all the women got up, "I hope everyone has an appetite this morning." Ssophia smiled at him as he began handing out the meals making sure the two little ones got their share. Clair spoke, "Thank you for preparing breakfast Gahe. Now we need to figure out how we are going to get Dannona and Tinne home." Resrassira said, "I can back track their route and we should be able to find their village, hopefully on the way they will see something familiar to help us."

After breakfast Clair told Gahe, "I want you to stay here just in case any of the drones return before they are due back. I am taking a radio with us and if something happen and we will need you to come rescue us with the shuttle." Gahe replied, "I would prefer to go with you but I understand and will follow your orders." All the girls took weapons with them; each had a pistol except for Resrassira she took a proton rifle. They made their way back to where Resrassira and Ssophia had found the girls and began back tracking from there. After an hour of tracking the group finally arrived at Dannona and Tinne's village.

As they entered the village they were met by a large crowd with several of them holding weapons, that is when the two girls ran out to meet the crowd telling them that these were their friends, they had save them and fed them. The crowd gathered around the two girls listening; all but three who were still staring at the group with their weapons ready. Finally an older man walked out to greet them, "I am Yidrach the elder of the village I would like to apologize for meeting you with weapon but we have to be cautious. Please come and let us thank you for taking care of our little ones." He then led them to his hut and asked them in, then turned to one of the girls in the room, "Bring food and drinks for our honored guest." Marjori spoke up, "Please we are fine we just wanted to make sure Dannona and Tinne made it home safe, I know their parents had to be worried." The elder lowered his head, "That they were; we all thought the Rutodrog had gotten them and they were gone forever."

Marjori thought for a moment then asked, "What is a Rutodrog?" The elder replied, "It is a large hairy beast that has plagues our village for years, it comes in from the forest and kills our animals carrying them off to eat and sometime our villagers." She asked, "How often does this happen." The elder replied about once a month and it is getting close to

53

that time and that is why we thought the girls were gone for good." He continued, "We never know when it will show it could be day or night."

Marjori then looked over to the others, "We need to get back to the shuttle we left Gahe alone and that creator could show up there." She told the elder, "We need to leave we left someone alone back at our camp and he could be in danger." Before the girls could get out of the elders house there was screaming from outside and a girl came in yelling, "The Rutodrog is here!" Marjori looked over as Clair, "We have to do something." They ran outside and Clair shouted, "Marjori you Ssophia and I will distract it with small fire from our pistols, Resrassira you find a location to get a good shot on it and take it down." Resrassira nodded, "Sounds like a good plan, I'm on it."

While the villagers were panicking and the men were shooting arrows at it as the girls got into position. They begin firing their pistols and were doing a great job distracting the beast. Resrassira crawled on top of one of the low level buildings and took aim with the rifle then with one single head shot brought the beast to the ground. The elder walked over to the beast and kicked it and after seeing there was no movement he turned to the villagers, "The beast is dead, no more living in fear." Everyone broke in to cheers as the elder walked over to the women to thank them for saving their village. The villagers wanted to have a huge party to celebrate and wanted the four of them to stay for the celebration, but Clair said, "We thank you for the invitation but we have a team member still out there alone we need to get back to." The elder lowered his head, "I understand, but thank you for your courage my village can now live in peace and you are welcome back anytime."

As the group was getting ready to head back to the shuttle Dannona and Tinne came running out, they gave everyone a hug and a necklace made of beads and a wild Bewa's tooth, it seemed the Bewa was a large canine that roamed the forest. They made their way back through the forest and to the shuttle where Gahe was sitting worrying about the four of them. He stood up and wiped the sweat from his head, "I am so happy to see the four of you back safe, did you get our two lovely guests home safely?" Ssophia smiled at him, "Yes they made it back home safely and so did we, you can stop worrying now."

Gahe replied, "I wasn't worried I knew you all could take care of yourselves." Clair put her hand on his shoulder as she walked by, "Sure you did, but thanks for worrying about us." Gahe just set down, "Ok I was worried, but we don't know anything about this planet." Ssophia kissed him on the cheek, "Again that is why I love you."

Later that evening the drones started returning and everyone pitched in gathering them and packing them up for the trip back to the Seeker. After everything was onboard Clair fired the engines up, Ssophia made them invisible and they made their way up through the atmosphere and headed toward the asteroid belt.

While the southern team was dealing with the Rutodrog, the team up north was dealing with snow, they had gotten up the next morning buried in snow that had blown in under the overhang and covered half the shuttle. They had spent all day digging the shuttle out and finished just in time for the drones to return. They collected all the drone packed them up and lifted off heading home.

Clair's team got back ten minutes before Dargon's and the cargo team had already unloaded the drone crate. Dargon brought his shuttle in to land and as soon as the ramp was down the cargo team was there to unload their drone crate. As they were leaving the shuttle Mouse told the cargo team to just leave the crates next to the shuttles he would be back later to pull the data. As Clair's team were leaving the shuttle bay she shouted to Dargon, "Get cleaned up Caalin wants us in the briefing room in an hour to fill him in on everything we encountered." Dargon shouted back, "Ok see you in an hour."

# CHAPTER 10

||||||||||||||||||||||||||||||||||||||||||||

# BACK FROM KRITILIA

After an hour everyone made their way to the briefing room where Caalin, Jason, Ang, Jean, and Rostrik were already waiting to hear about the survey. Everyone made their way to their seats and Caalin looked over at them, "Ok who would like to go first and tell me how things went." Clair turned to Dargon, "You should go first since you were in charge of the entire survey." Dargon smiled, "Thank you I will." Dargon went into detail about how they landed at the first location that he and Caalin picked out and it was a good location to prevent any surveillance from over head. He paused, "We did not have any issues until later in the evening when a snow storm rowed in and buried us in snow. We barely got the area cleared the next day before the drones started returning, but other than the storm everything went off without a hitch and we are just waiting on Mouse to show up with the data."

Caalin turned to Clair, "And how did things go for your team?" Clair replied, "Well the landing and getting the shuttle under cover went great. We secured the area and launched the drones with no issues." She paused, "But that evening we felt we were being watch so Ssophia and Resrassira went out to see who was watching us." Caalin asked, "I take it they went unseen?" Ssophia smile, "You know we did, you wouldn't have had it any other way would you?" Caalin chuckled, "No, Sorry please continue Clair." Clair continued, "Well after a few minutes the two of them returned accompanied by two lovely little girls; I would say they were around seven or eight years of age."

Caalin looked a little shocked, "So this planet is inhabited?" Clair replied, "Yes and we got to meet a village filled with people." Caalin came back with, "Ok explain how you came about meeting the village." Clair continued the story, "Well the two girls had gotten lose so they spent the night with us and the next morning Marjori, Ssophia, Resrassira and myself decided to get them home to their parents." Marjori jumped in, "It was thanks to Resrassira's tracking skills that we were able to find their trail back to the village." Clair continued, "The villagers were a little wary of us until the girls explained to them we had kept them safe and fed them, that is when the village elder welcomed us. He told us they thought the girls had been eaten by a creator they called a Rutodrog, and as he was telling us about how the beast terrorizes the village killing their animals and villagers, the creator attacked." She lowered her head, "We had no chose but to take the creator down to prevent anyone being killed." Marjori jumped back in, "After that the village thanked us and wanted us to stay for a celebration but we explained that we had left someone back at our camp and needed to get back. When we got back the drones were returning so we packed everything up and made it home safe and sound."

Caalin set quietly thinking about what he had just heard then looked over at Clair's team, "Well you had no other chose but to put that beast down and I am proud of you all, unfortunately we do not have time to set up relations with the village because of our mission, but hopefully we can in the future." All the girls on Clair's team were smiling and Clair thanked Caalin for his comment. It was about that time Mouse came into the briefing room, "Sorry I am late but I have all the data from the drones, I thought you may want to see it so I stayed behind to pull it."

Caalin turned to Mouse, "Well let's hear what you found out." Mouse smiled, "It would be better if I show you." He brought up the holographic map of the planet but this time it had all the new data add to it. He pointed to all the marked locations on the map, "Those are all small villages scattered all around the planet. There was one just ten kilometers from our location and one even closer to Clair's location." Caalin cleared his throat, "We know about Clair's village but the big question is if there is any sign of pirate activity on the planet." Mouse was a little puzzled from the comment but answered, "No not a single sign of any pirate activity, there were no ships of any size on the planet other than ours."

Caalin stood up, "Well that is good news, everyone get some rest we will start preparing for our next mission to Raitora tomorrow." Everyone got up and was leaving the room and Ang made her way over to join Ssophia, Clair and Marjori, "I want to hear more about those two little girls." Ssophia giggled, "You would have loved them; they were so cute. They even gave us all necklaces to thank us." Ang looked at her necklace, "I am so jealous that is the cutest thing that I've seen in some time." Ssophia leaned over and whispered, "Cuter than the one bracelet Caalin gave you?" Ang gave her a look, "NO, but it is pretty dang close."

Caalin caught Dargon before he walked out, "I think the next planet we each will take a team and leave Clair in charge of the ship, so think about it tonight and let me know who you would like to be in your group then I will select mine. Dargon stopped and thought for a moment, "I will take Ssam, Mouse, Sisten and Rostrik, I don't have to think about it long, if this is the planet with pirates I want people I can count on, besides you can handle anything that comes your way." Caalin put his hand on Dargon's shoulder, "If that's the team you want then I am fine with it, but do sell yourself short, you are great at handling things as they come up."

Later at dinner Ang and Ssophia joined Caalin and his table and Ang asked, "Ok who are you taking on your team, we ran into Dargon and know who is going down with him." Caalin looked at the two girls, "Gahe, Ssophia, Faelara and Aeron." Ang looked disappointed, "I can guess why you picked them, Gahe you need to handle the drones, Ssophia you need to get to the planet unseen and she is also your medical support, and you picked both Faelara and Aeron as security because you think this may be the planet that could be trouble." Caalin shook his head, "And again you read my mind, but I would not be taking Ssophia if I didn't need her for the trip down, I would have selected Jean for the medical support and the fact that she has more military experience."

Ssophia laughed, "I am just a stealth generator for him, it is just lucky that I am also part of the medical crew." That comment got Caalin thinking, "You know what on second thought I don't think I will take Ssophia." Both of the girls looked and him, and in unison, "What do you mean?" Caalin smiled maybe we don't need two shuttles to go down maybe we can do it with one of the larger shuttles." He stood up, "I will see you later I need to go talk to Dargon." Ang shouted to him as he was walking off, "Wait you didn't finish your meal!" He looked back at her, "I can't think about eating now I've got work to do."

As Caalin was leaving the dining hall Mouse was just arriving, "Mouse, come with me I need to talk to you and Dargon." Mouse mumbled, "OK but I was about to get something to eat." Caalin replied, "This should not take long but I need to discuss it with the two of you before we do anything else." The two of them reached the bridge just in time to catch Dargon before he left. Dargon asked, "Caalin I wasn't expecting you back on the bridge tonight." Caalin replied, "I wasn't planning on coming back but I need to talk with you, come to the briefing room."

Once the three of them were in the briefing room Caalin turned, "One shuttle, we are only using one shuttle for the next mission." Dargon asked, "Why one shuttle?" Caalin answered, "This is the last planet and it is possible this is where the pirate could have a strong hold. I don't want to endanger more people than I have to so we are taking one shuttle." Mouse put his hand on his chin, "Oh I get it you we are going to land somewhere near the equator and you want me to reprogram the drones to go from there." Caalin pointed at Mouse, "That is correct." He then pulled up the map of Raitora and said, "Ok let's see if we can find a good location to land." The three of them began staring at the map and watching the equator as it rotated in front of them. Dargon stopped the map from rotating and pointed to a small volcanic island, "Right there, it looks like a large lava tube big enough to get one of the larger shuttles in, but we may have to back it into the tube." Caalin pulled the image up as large as he could, "It looks like it will be a tight fit, but I think it will do."

Mouse nodded his head, "Ok I will reprogram the drones to launch from the equator and return to whatever location we launch them from, but we will be down there for more than two days, this is a larger planet than the other two." Dargon turned to Caalin, "With this change I suspect you already know who you want to go on this mission." Caalin smiled, "I sure do, it will be you and I, Mouse, Ssam, Rostrik, Faelara and Aeron; we will be taking Jean as our medical person. I want people who will be an asset if we run into any problem." Dargon looked over at

Caalin, "Let me guess we are taking Captain Anderson not only because she can handle any medical issues but for her military experience as well." Caalin looked at Dargon, "You have got to stop reading my mind, Ang and Ssophia do that enough, but yes you are right."

Caalin turned to Mouse, "How long will it take you to reprogram the drones?" Mouse smiled, "What time are we having our briefing tomorrow?" Caalin asked, "15:00 why?" Mouse laughed, "Plenty of time, they will be ready at 13:00 and loaded on the shuttle by 14:00, that is if you know which shuttle we are taking." Caalin thought for a moment, "How about AS1-S3, I will let Marty know to have his team check it out." Mouse started toward the door, "Ok they will be programmed and on the shuttle by 14:00 tomorrow, now I am going to get something to eat." Caalin said, "Wait a minute and I will go with you, I didn't get a chance to eat my dinner earlier." Dargon jumped in, "Well if you two are heading to the dinning hall I will join you, I could use something to eat too." Mouse slapped his head, "We could have just had our talk over dinner." They were all laughing as they walked out of the briefing room.

# CHAPTER 11

|||||||||||||||||||||||||||||||||||||||||||||||||||

# PREP FOR RAITORA

The next morning Ang joined Caalin for breakfast and while they were enjoying the meal she asked, "Well have you changed your mind about the personnel for the next survey mission?" He smiled at her, "No, and you are still not on this one." She looked at him seriously, "I know Ssophia and I are being left behind because you think the pirates may have a base on this planet and you want us out of harm's way. Well Mr. Matthews that is not going to stop me from worrying about you while you are gone, you seem to get into a lot of trouble when we aren't around." Caalin replied, "Well that might be a little true, but at least I know the two of you are safer here on the Seeker."

Their conversation was cut short when Mouse showed up with Sisten, "Caalin I just wanted to let you know that the drones have been reprogrammed and Marty's team is getting them loaded onto the shuttle this morning. We could actually leave earlier for our mission if you would like." Caalin thought for a moment, "That sounds like a good Idea, I will get with Dargon and we can call everyone for a briefing for 10:00, which would allow us a departure time of 15:00 putting us on the planet in plenty of time to launch the drones before dark." Mouse came back with, "We will be on the planet a little longer because it will take the drones fifty hours to complete the survey. That would mean if we land at 15:30 it will take about thirty minutes to deploy the drones so they will not return until around 18:00 two days later."

Caalin stood up, "Well I had better head to the bridge and set up the briefing." Mouse turned to him, "Ok I will see you at the 10:00 briefing, I have some research I need to do in engineering before the meeting." Mouse told Sisten he would see her later and headed off toward engineering. As Mouse was walking off Ang looked at Sisten, "Well it looks like we both were abandon; would you care to join me for breakfast?" Sisten smiled, "Sure I would love to." The two of them were soon joined by Ssophia and the three of them enjoyed their breakfast while talking about the boys."

Caalin reached the bridge and took a seat, he then informed Dargon that they would be heading down to Raitora at 15:00 instead of waiting to the next morning so he needed everyone in the briefing room at 10:00 for the briefing. Dargon quickly walked over and gave Asgaya the names of all the individuals that needed to be at the briefing besides the usual officers. Asgaya nodded her head, "I will contact them right away."

Soon it was briefing time and Caalin was watching everyone as they enter the room, "Please everyone take a seat and get comfortable." Once everyone was seated Caalin began, "As everyone knows this is the last of the three planets we have to survey; chances are that if the pirates have a strong hold in this Nebula it would be on this planet since we found no signs of them on the other two. Because of this we are only taking one shuttle down and will be on the planet a little longer than the last two missions. The personnel I have picked for this mission are: Dargon, Ssam for navigation and stealth, Mouse to handle the drones, Rostrik,

Faelara, and Aeron for security, and Jean for medical support and also for her military experience; I also will be on this mission as well."

He then looked over to Jason and Clair, "The two of you are in charge of the Seeker, I want her on high alert while we are away just in case anything happens and we cannot get back to the ship we will get you the information you need and you are to get out of this asteroid field and jump back to Alliance space giving them the information." He then addressed the others, "Ok those that are going with me down to the planet take care of anything you need to take care of and meet Dargon and me in the shuttle bay at 15:00; you all are dismissed."

As everyone was leaving Jean walked over to Caalin, "I am glad you have included me in this mission, are you expecting trouble this time?" Caalin looked at her seriously, "Not expecting any, just preparing for the worst case scenario." Jean patted him on the shoulder, "Now that is thinking like a true captain of an Alliance cruiser." Caalin smiled, "Thanks but I was just thinking about the safety of the people I care about." Jean smiled back, "I know."

As Caalin walked out of the briefing room Belrion was there waiting for him, "I just wanted you to know I will make sure plenty of food has been loaded on the shuttle for you and it also includes emergency rations should the worst happen and you can't make it back to the ship." Caalin smiled at him, "Thank you for think ahead and taking care of everyone, and I am not just talking about the ones going with me on this mission." Belrion lowered his head, "I understand and my team is happy to serve under your command, they all love working on board because you go out of your way to make us feel like family." Caalin put his hand on Belrion's shoulder, "I am not going out of my way, I consider your entire team as part of my family and I am very grateful for each one of them."

Dargon walked up after over hearing the conversation, "Now what is up with the two of you are acting like we are not making it back from this mission, so knock it off we don't want to worry everyone."

Caalin turned to Dargon, "You are right, no need to think the worst is going to happen when we have no idea if the pirates are on that planet or not." He continued, "Well I am heading to my room to prepare myself to head down to the planet and I would suggest you get ready as well, we only have a few hours." With that Belrion left heading back to the kitchen as Dargon and Caalin headed off to their rooms.

Later Caalin went by the medical facility to see if Ang wanted to have lunch with him, but there was no one around so he made his way up to the dining hall. As he came through the door he saw everyone at a large table setup along the back wall. Ang waved at him to come over and as he got closer she told him that since they did not know what might happen on this mission everyone wanted to have lunch together before he and his team left for the planet. He smiled at her, "That's a great idea." He took his seat next to her as Orianna came around to see what Caalin would like to eat. Caalin looked up at her, "Whatever the special is today that would be fine with me, I know no matter what it is it will be great." She smiled, "Yes sir today's special coming right up."

Everyone set around the table telling stories from school and when they were on the Abolefacio, laughing and having a good time. After lunch Caalin walked Ang back down to the medical facility and gave her a kiss to thank her for setting up the lunch group. Before he could walk off she grabbed him and hugged him tightly, "Don't you do anything foolish while you are down on Raitora I want to see you back on board the day after tomorrow." Caalin whispered in her ear, "I will do my best to stay out of trouble, but I can't guarantee that trouble won't find us."

A tear ran down her eye as she replied, "I know but do your best, I can't deal with the thought of loosing you again."

Caalin kissed her once again then turned and made his way toward the bridge. Once on the bridge he again went over what he expected Jason and Clair to do if something goes crazy down on Raitora. Clair looked at Caalin, "I am not happy with those orders; I don't want to go through what I did when I thought I had loss Ssam so you had better make sure you bring everyone back safely." Ssam over heard the comment, "Caalin will do his best to make sure everyone gets back, he is not one to leave anyone behind." Clair turned, "I know and he is only thinking about everyone that will be left on the ship but I don't have to be happy with it."

Caalin looked at the two of them, "I know this puts a big burden on both of you, but for the sake of everyone on board I expect you to follow those orders." Jason replied, "No matter if we agree with you on this one we will do it for everyone on board, but I would prefer you get back safely so we don't have to follow those orders." Caalin put his hand on Jason's shoulder, "That is the plan, we are just preparing for the worst case scenario." It was getting close to the departure time and Caalin made his way down to the shuttle bay. While waiting on the rest of his team he looked over everything they had on board the shuttle and verified it was all secure. He then went out to meet the rest of the team.

He got everyone together before boarding the shuttle to go over the plan for the mission. He cleared his throat, "Ok this is how it should go, today is day one; we travel down to the planet to our selected landing location and secure the shuttle. Mouse, Aeron and Dargon will deploy the drones while the rest of us secure the perimeter. Day two we will scout the area around us to see if there is anything in the area that may be a problem. Day three we continue scouting while waiting on the return of the drones and once they return we pack up and head home. Hopefully this will be a boring trip with nothing to report."

After Caalin concluded his talk everyone boarded the shuttle for takeoff. Caalin moved to the pilot seat and Dargon to the copilot seat while Ssam took a front row seat next to the bulkhead so he could place his hand on it to make them invisible. The shuttle lifted off and slowly made its way off the ship and into the asteroid field. Caalin maneuver the shuttle through the asteroids and as they were leaving the field Ssam did his thing and they vanished.

# CHAPTER 12
‖‖‖‖‖‖‖‖‖‖‖‖‖‖‖‖‖‖‖‖‖‖‖‖‖‖‖‖‖‖‖‖‖‖‖
# LAST MISSION RAITORA

Soon they were entering the atmosphere and making their way down to the equator, and Caalin took the shuttle along the equator until it reached the tropical island that was covered with lava tubes from the time it was an active volcano. Maneuvering it along the cliff of the now extinct volcano he came to the large tube so he turned the shuttle around and moved it backward into the tube. The shuttle reappeared and the ramp slowly opened with Rostrik and Faelara exiting first to make sure the area was secure.

Once the all clear was given, Dargon, Ssam, Mouse and Aeron began moving the containers with the drones out of the shuttle and started placing them on the ground at the entrance of the tube. Within thirty minutes the drones were lifting off the ground and on their way out of the lave tube to complete their mission. Jean setup a small research table and had started taking algae from the walls of the lava tube to run tests to see what it was made up of. Caalin and Aeron decided to fly down to the tropical jungle below to see what wild life if any was there. Rostrik and Faelara decided to setup parameter sensors, while Mouse was looking at schematics on the computer still working on creating a generator to connect to the shield generator that would give them stealth capability. Dargon and Ssam decided to take it easy and set back to relax their time away.

Caalin and Aeron found bird like creators nesting among the trees and crustaceans crawling along the shore line. After circling the island for a few hours the two of them decided to return back to the shuttle since it was slowly getting darker. Once back at the shuttle they setup sleeping areas outside of the shuttle leaving the inside for Faelara and Jean. Caalin and Aeron quickly returned to the jungle long enough to pick up some fire wood and then flew right back. They started a small fire underneath a small lave tube going up so that the smoke created would flow up out of the large tube. Ssam setup some lights around the area so they would be able to see should anyone want to wonder around the area. Later they had their dinner and set around talking until settling in for the night.

The next morning Caalin and Aeron decided to fly to the top of the extinct volcano to see what they could find. When they reached the top the crater was full of water the slowly spilt of the edge running down the back side creating some small waterfalls. Caalin flew up about the edge of the crater and looking all around he could see two smaller islands not far from their location. The two of them decided to fly over to the closes island and take a look around. They soared back down the cliff, out over the jungle and across the water to the first small island. They made their way all around the island finding out that it was not much different than the one they were on so they called it quits for the day and headed back.

The rest of the day consisted of Dargon and Ssam exploring deeper into the lava tube, Mouse still going over his schematics, Jean with her research, Rostrik and Faelara sitting at the entrance to the lava tube staring out over the jungle below. Aeron and Caalin just kicked back and took a nap since they were both tired from their exploring. After dinner that evening everyone sat around talking until deciding to go to bed.

The next day they spent the morning packing everything up so they would be prepared to leave once the drones returned that evening. Later after lunch Caalin and Aeron left to check out the last little island while everyone else stayed back setting around waiting on the drones. The two of them reached the second small island late in the afternoon and started their exploration. After a while of wondering through the jungle Caalin spotted what looked like an antenna sticking up through the trees but as he got closer he spotted some of the drones heading back to the shuttle. He turned to Aeron, "It looks like the drones have began returning so we need to head back, but before we leave I want to see what that is, it looks like an antenna of some kind."

As the two of them got closer to the antenna they could see a small building with dishes mounted along the roof, and before Aeron could warn Caalin one of the dishes turned in his direction and a light began to blink on top of it. Aeron pointed it out to Caalin, "I think we have triggered something, we may want to get out of here and get off the planet as quickly as possible." Caalin nodded, "I think you are right about that, let's move." The two of them moved back through the juggle as fast as they could until they reached a clearing and took off flying over the trees and water back to the others.

As they returned to the shuttle Dargon greeted them, "Well all the drones made it back earlier than we thought and we have them loaded onboard." Caalin replied, "That's great we need to leave now, we think we may have triggered an alarm on that other island." Everyone boarded the shuttle and Caalin turned to Ssam, "Make us vanish as quick as you can once we are out of this tube, not before I want to make sure we don't hit any walls so I need to be able to see the exterior on the way out." Ssam nodded, "You got it once we are clear the tube we vanish."

Caalin took the shuttle out slowly but as they exited the tube two fighter ships appeared in the sky above them. One of the fighters spotted them and fired hitting the portside rear exhaust vent causing the plasma core to fluctuate and not allowing Caalin to go to full throttle. Mouse shouted, "I will take care of the plasma core, Ssam you need to make us vanish." Ssam put his hand on the wall and they vanished while Mouse ran back and pulled the cover from the plasma generator. Mouse could see that the blast they took jarred the plasma connector loose so he quickly reconnected it, but although they were invisible there was still some smoke coming from the exhaust vents. The smoke allowed the second fighter to hit them with another shot which caused the shuttle to jerk.

The Shuttle jerking caused Mouse to lose his balance and fall forward into the plasma generator where his left arm went directly into the plasma field disintegrating it all the way up to his shoulder. Mouse let out a scream and pushed his self backwards away from the generator as he shouted to Caalin, "It is fixed get us out of here!" Once Mouse hit the floor he passed out from shock. Jean quickly grabbed a medical pack and rushed to his side, hooking it up to him and checking all his vital signs. She looked at his arm and to her surprise the nanos in Mouse's system had already sealed the wound and stopped the bleeding. Jean told Caalin, "Mouse is going to be ok, he is just in shock but we need to get to the ship and get him to the medical facility."

Caalin took the shuttle higher through the atmosphere until they were in space, but the fighters were still on their trail and he could detect a cruiser heading in their direction. He looked over at Dargon, "I don't think Ssam's power is going to keep them from detecting us once that cruiser gets closer we need to let the Seeker know to get out of here." Dargon sent the message, "Seeker this is AS1-S3 we are being pursued, you need to abandon us and leave the system. Once out of the system send a message to the Alliance, if we can get to the asteroid field we may be able to hold out until help arrives."

Clair's voice came over the intercom, "AS1-S3 I have received your command and unwillingly we will carry them out so do your best to hold out." With that the Seeker unlocked its self from the asteroid they had been sitting on the entire time they were in the system, it slowly moved out of the asteroid field and once out did a dimensional jump. Dargon turned to Caalin, "They are gone; do you think we have a chance to make it to the asteroid field?"

Caalin looked back at Mouse laying unconscious, "If Mouse was still conscious I would say yes because he would have gave us enough power to do it, but with what power we have right now it is a fifty-fifty chance." Dargon gave a half hearted smile, "Well at lease it is not a zero chance."

The shuttle was getting closer to the asteroid field but unfortunately the cruiser and the fighters were getting closer to them as well and it was looking like they were not going to make it. Caalin turned to the others, "Hang on this may get bumpy ride if we make it at all." No sooner had Caalin made that comment the Seeker suddenly reappeared firing on the two fighters taking them out and then turning its attention on the cruiser. A voice came over the intercom, "We have returned to get you, so get that shuttle on board now." The Seeker turned to expose the shuttle bay opening for them and Caalin brought the shuttle in for a rough landing, skidding in across the bay floor and into one of the smaller shuttles.

The Seeker then jumped again leaving the system and fast as it could. The shuttle doors opened and Jean was yelling, "Get a stretcher we have an injured crewmember!" Marty's team jump in fast and was there with a stretcher before they had Mouse off the shuttle. They rushed Mouse straight to the medical facility while Caalin, Dargon and Ssam ran straight to the bridge. Once on the bridge Caalin asked Clair why did she disobey his order to leave them and get the Seeker out of harm's way? Clair just looked him straight in the eyes, "Captain Matthews we did follow your orders and left, but your orders did not say we could not return after we left." There was a tear running down her cheek, "We could not leave people we care about behind."

Caalin then gave her a hug, "My entire team thanks you for amending my orders." He then looked over a Mari who was on navigation, "Mari where did we jump to?" She looked at the system, "I have no idea we just did a random jump and the computer has not calculated the location yet, but it seems we are pretty close to a blackhole." Caalin turn to Ssam, "Take over navigation we don't know if that cruiser can track us and we need to be prepared and you know what we need to do." Caalin took the captain's seat, "Take us toward the blackhole." Ssam navigated them closer and closer to the hole and Caalin's fears came true as the cruise suddenly appeared behind them. Caalin told Ssam, "Get us as close as you can then jump, don't forget to mark the jump locations." Ssam nodded, "I got this under control."

The cruiser began getting closer and began firing on them, as Caalin told Ssam, "OK jump in ten." Ssam began counting down the seconds until just, "10, 9, 8, 7, 6, 5, 4,3,2,1 jumping." But just as he jumped they were hit by one of the shots from the cruiser, and although it did damage it did not interrupt the jump and they completed it with no issues. Unfortunately once they came out of the jump all the engines went off line, all they had were propulsion jets to maneuver the ship with. Gahe came over the intercom, "Caalin the engines have taken a lot of damage and I have no idea how long it is going to take to get them back up, all we can do now is drift." Caalin stood up, "Clair you have the bridge, Dargon, Ssam lets go down to see if we can help in engineering."

After a couple of hours helping Gahe and Jon in engineering it looked like they had enough parts to get the impulse drive back up and running but they would not be able to bring the jump drive back on line and that included the dimensional communication system. Caalin turn to the group, "Well if we get impulse back up maybe we can find a planet where we can find all the parts we need to fix the Jump drive." He scratched his head, 'Ok let's start on the impulse engine once we have it back up we can see what we need to repair the jump system." The four of them began working with Marty and his team helping them by retrieving the part they needed as they asked for them.

# CHAPTER 13

||||||||||||||||||||||||||||||||||||||||||||||

# APPEARANCE OF A CARGO FREIGHTER AND HELP

Caalin, Dargon, Ssam, Gahe and Jon had been working on the impulse engine all night and it still was not working for them. Caalin told everyone let's take a break grab breakfast and get a little rest maybe we will get it working once we have eaten and have clear heads. They all move to the dining hall and were eating when Clair came in to inform Caalin that a cargo ship had just appeared off their starboard side and was asking if they needed any assistance. Caalin and Dargon quickly finished their meal and went to the bridge, once there Caalin looked at the monitor and could see that the cargo ship was huge. He contact the ship, "This is Caalin Matthews captain of the AS1-Seeker may I ask who you are?" The voice came back this is the Cargo Ship Igashu and we were in route to deliver some cargo when we came across your ship. You were setting dead in space so we wanted to know if we could assist you in any way. We do have an excellent engineering team and a lot of parts that may help in getting you going again."

Caalin was thinking about the situation when the voice asked, "May we send two liaison officers over to discuss your situation and see how we may be of assistance." Caalin replied, "Yes send you liaison over and we will discuss things with them when they arrive." No sooner had Caalin said that a small shuttle left the Igashu and moved in their direction." Caalin told Clair, inform Marty's team we have guest coming over, I am heading down to greet them." Caalin then left running all the way down to the shuttle bay and arrive just as the small shuttle was setting down in the hanger.

The small shuttle landed and two lovely girls exited and walked over to meet Caalin. One of the girls had wings, green eyes and teal green hair and the other had blonde hair and bright blue eyes. The winged girl spoke, "We are the liaisons from the Igashu, you can call me Jill and this is Lea, it is a pleasure to meet you." Caalin started to introduce himself when Lea leaned over and whispered, "We know who you are and we are here to help you get back to your time." Caalin was shocked and quickly told the two of them, "Come with me so we can talk in private." He led them up to his room and asked them in, once inside he took them into his personal office and told them to have a seat. He then set down at his desk, "OK, how do you know who we are, and that we are not from this time."

Jill spoke, "That we cannot tell you about it could cause a big rift in time, but we do know that the help we can give you will not affect the time line at all, we just ask that you trust us." Caalin looked at the two girls, "If I trust you none of my crew can know that we are not in our time, there are only a few people here that know that information." Lea replied, "We know that it is not only you that know but Ssamuel Ssallazz and his sister Ssophia, Angiliana Avora and Mortomous Valtor who has lost his left arm." Jill smiled, "Captain Matthews we are only here to help and nothing else, so please let us help you."

Caalin set back in his chair thinking, then he spoke, "Ok, I will ask no further questions and trust you. Our impulse engine and our jump systems are all down so we could use all the help you can give us." Jill stood up, "Great sir, now if you would let us we will tow the Seeker onboard the Igashu and assist with all the repairs." She then pulled out a small communications device and said, "Igashu this is Jill please have the two large shuttles removed from bay six zero three and send two tow ships over to tow the Seeker into that bay." Caalin could hear the voice from the other side reply, "Will do, the shuttles will be moved out and dock on the port side, and the two tow shuttles are on their way."

Caalin stood up, "Well if we are being towed over we need to make our way to the bridge so I can inform the crew." The three of them left his quarters and made their way to the bridge where Caalin introduced the two girls as just Jill and Lea. He then asked Keyan to open ship wide communications so he could address the crew. Once she had the line open Caalin announced, "I want to let everyone know we are about to be towed onto the cargo ship Igashu where they will be assisting us with repairs to the Seeker, I ask that everyone welcome the crew that come onboard to help and treat them with respect, which I already know you will."

Caalin and the two girls then made their way down to engineering and informed the team there that the Igashu engineer team will be there to help and they will also bring parts for them to fix everything. He then pulled Ssam to the side, "These two girls know everything about us and our time travel so don't let Dargon or anyone ask the engineer team coming over to many questions that may lead to them figuring it out." Ssam looked puzzled, "How do they know about us?" Caalin replied, "I don't know myself but they assure me that all the help they give us will not affect the time line so we will have to trust them on that."

Once the Seeker was locked down in bay six zero three of the Igashu the engineers, from the Igashu, begin boarding bring with them carts of parts to help with the repairs. Dargon and Ssam greeted them and led them to engineering where Jon and Gahe were still working. The Igashu engineers just fell right in with them and began helping with all the repairs.

Jill had one of the Igashu's crew members move the small shuttle they had arrived on off the Seeker and back into the Igashu's cargo shuttle bay. While Caalin and the two girls were watching him moving the shuttle Ang came running up to talk to Caalin. Jill looked around, "Angiliana nice to meet you, you're here to let Captain Matthews know that your cousin has come to and wants to leave the medical facility to help with the ship repairs despite the fact that he only has one arm now." Ang stopped dead in her tracks; she looked shocked and asks Caalin, "How does she know that?" Caalin quickly pull Ang and the other two girls off to the side so they could not be over heard, and then explained everything to Ang about the two girls.

Lea looked over to Jill, "I think it is time to take him to see Matthew don't you?" Jill nodded her head, "Yes Matthew will take good care of him." Ang looked at the two girls, "Take who to Matthew, and who is this Matthew you are talking about." Jill put her hand up to her mouth, "Oh I'm sorry, Matthew is our medical engineer, he is into bionics and can take care of Mortomous' missing arm." Caalin looked at her, "Do you mean he could build Mouse a new arm?" Jill replied, "Yes and I am sure he has one that will work for him already." Caalin looked at Ang, "What are we waiting for let's get Mouse and get him over to see this Matthew guy."

Caalin and the three girls made their way up to the medical facility where Mouse was still trying to talk Ssophia and Sisten to let him leave so he could help in engineering. As the four of them walked into the medical facility Caalin looked over at Mouse, "Ok ladies you can let him go he is coming with us." He then turned to Ang, "You can explain it to the two of them we don't have time to waste." He grabbed Mouse by the one arm he had left and the two of them follow Jill and Lea out and down off the Seeker.

Once on the Igashu the girl took them to an elevator and they went up several floors until it finally stopped. Once the doors open the girls led Caalin and Mouse to a medical lab where a man stood on the other side of the room tinkering with something on a table. Jill spoke up; "Matthew he is here so you need to do your thing." The young man turned around and Caalin was surprised by how much he looked like Mouse, with the exception of his hair and eye color, his hair was black and his eyes were blue.

Matthew looked at the two girls, "I have it ready now, and all we need to do is attack it." He then turned to Mouse, "If you will just lie down on this table we will begin attaching the arm." Mouse looked at Caalin, "What is going on around here?" Caalin replied, "We are getting you a new arm to replace the one you lose, now just trust us and I will explain everything to you afterwards." Mouse still not sure of it all, "Ok I will trust you but this is a lot for me to take in." Caalin put his hand on his shoulder, "Don't worry pal it will all be fine."

Matthew connected what looked like an IV to Mouse's arm, "These are nanos, you have a lot of different nanos in your system already but not like these, they will help your other ones control the arm and can produce synthetic skin to cover the arm so it will look just like a real arm." He then brought the bionic arm over and fitted it on to what was left of Mouse's missing arm. As soon as he had it in place the nanos inside Mouse's body began to take over and started wiring his nervous system into the synthetic nerve system of the arm. Matthew told Mouse, "Once this is complete you will actually be able to feel things with the arm, if you touch something or something brushes up against the arm you will feel it just like the arm you are missing."

While Caalin and Matthew were over with Mouse, Jill and Lea were standing off to the side just watching and Jill was heard saying, "He was extremely handsome when he was young, I can see why Angiliana use to get jealous." After about two hours the procedure was complete and the new arm was attached. Matthew looked at Mouse, "Ok let's test it, open and close your hand." Mouse opened and closed his hand and it felt like it was his original hand, like the accident never happened. He looked at Matthew, "This feels great, just like my original arm, I can't tell the difference."

Matthew looked around the room then picked up a solid metal container, "Here squeezed this." He handed Mouse the container and Mouse gave it a squeezed crushing the container. Matthew then told him, "You see this one is a lot stronger so you will have to be very careful when applying pressure with it you could crush whatever you are squeezing, like Sisten's hand or worst." Mouse looked at the hand on his new arm, "I will be extremely careful thank you for the warning."

Jill then spoke up, "Well we need to get them back to their ship the repairs are all done and they have a mission to complete." Matthew shook both of their hands, "It was great to have met you even though it wasn't in your own time." Mouse looked at Caalin and Caalin just said, "I will explain it to you later." The girls took them back to the elevator and down to bay six zero three where the Seeker set waiting on their return. The two small tow shuttles were ready to tow them out of the bay so when Caalin and Mouse got back on board they turned and wave goodbye to Jill and Lea then the doors began to close.

The Two shuttles began moving the Seeker off of the Igashu and as they cleared the entrance to the bay the two shuttles that were moved to the port side were taken back on board. Once far enough out the tow shuttles released them and made their way back to the Igashu. No sooner had the tow shuttles gotten back on board the Igashu made a jump and was gone, but on board Jill and Lea was walking back into Matthew's lab. Jill looked over to Matthew, "Well how do you feel after helping you grandfather by replacing his missing arm." Matthew replied, "It was great, that man took great care of me when I spent time with him. He and grandmother are the reason I do what I do today and I know he will create another arm using mine as a template." Matthew then returned the question, "Well Jillian how was it for you and Leanna seeing your grandfather?" Jillian replied, "It was wonderful we even saw our grandmothers and your grandmother while on board." The three of them spent another two hours in Matthew's lab with Matthew saying, "It was due to the two of you going through your grandfather's diary and finding the Seekers old data files that we knew where to find them, even though it took us two tries to get the right location." Jill nodded, "Yeah, the star maps changed a little since their time, but we made it and they are on their way back." The three of them remained in Matthew's lab talking about their grandparents and laughing about the stories they had told them growing up.

On the Seeker Dargon reported that everything was up and functioning properly, they had even made improvements to the weapons system. Dargon then saw Mouse's arm, "How did you get a new arm, yours was completely gone." Mouse replied, "They had a great bionic engineer who replaced it with a bionic arm and it works great." Ssam walked over to Mouse, "One of the engineers gave me these crystals, he sad you would know what to do with them, they are azerithium crystals." Mouse shouted, "This is great, we cannot go anywhere until I complete something." He turned to Caalin, "We are about to go stealth so no jumps until I say we are ready." He then ran off toward engineering.

# CHAPTER 14

||||||||||||||||||||||||||||||||||||||||||||||||

# JUMP BACK UNSEEN

Mouse made it to engineering and pulled up his schematics for his stealth generator, lucky for him he had already built the biggest portion of it so all he needed to do is figure out how to mount the crystal in it to make it work. He was staring at the schematic then the generator and back to the schematic and did not even notice the four women behind him. Someone cleared their throat from behind him and he turned to see who it was and to his surprise there stood Sisten, Ssophia, Ang and Jean. Sisten gave Mouse an angry look, "Mr. Valtor why did you not come back to the medical facility once you returned to the ship." Mouse lowered his head, "I have something important I need to do first." He then held up his new arm, "But I am all good now so no need to go back to the medical facility."

Jean jumped back, "Is that a bionic arm, I knew the Alliance was working on them but I did not know there were any out there that looked that good." Mouse smiled, "This is a special one that was made just for me, the nanos in my body help me to control it and they produce the synthetic skin that covers it. Feel of it, it feels the same as my real skin." Sisten felt on the arm, "You're right I can't tell the difference, but you could have come by and let us know you were ok." Mouse lowered his head again, "I'm sorry, it will not happen again." Sisten pointed her finger at him, "It had better not; now come by after you're done with whatever you are doing we want to give you a complete check up." Before they walked off Jean said, "And I want to take a scan of that arm when you come by."

Mouse just waved saying, "Yeah, I will see you later." Then went back to working on the generator he was working on before they interrupted him. After an hour had passed Mouse had the stealth generator complete and ready to install, so he moved over to the force field power source and connected it into the system then routed it to a free switch on the control system. After the completion of the install he contact Caalin who was on the bridge with Dargon and Ssam, "I am ready to test the stealth generator so bring up the force field first." Caalin looked over at Ric who was setting in the navigation seat, "Bring the shields on line." Ric brought the force field up and everything was working so Mouse said, "Ok the switch just to the right of the shields is the stealth generator, hit that switch and bring it on line." Ric looked at Caalin and Caalin gave him the go ahead, Ric turned back and hit the switch and all of a sudden the Seeker disappeared.

Caalin informed Mouse that it was working great he had done an excellent job building it. Mouse laughed, "Now I will build some for the shuttles and then Ssam and Ssophia are out of the stealth business." Ssam shouted, "Great work, I was getting tired of that job anyway." Before Mouse could do anything else Caalin said, "Ok now you are done with that for now, you have an appointment in the medical facility so get there right away, and that's an order." Mouse replied back, "Yes sir I'm on my way." After that he headed off to the medical facility to get a complete physical.

Caalin turned to Ssam, "Take over navigation from Ric so he can man the port side cannons; Dargon you take the forward cannons and Clair the starboard cannons. Jason will you man the rear cannons just in case we need them." Jason replied, "I will but what are we about to do that we would need them?" Caalin answered, "We are about to make a jump and I want people on the guns in case we run into pirates after the jump." Everyone was ready and Caalin told Ssam, "Bring up the shields and the new stealth generator, then prepare to jump on my command." Ssam replied, "Shields up, stealth activated, and I have the jump programmed in, waiting on your command." Caalin announced over the ship wide intercom, "We are about to jump, we may encounter pirate activity when we come out of the jump so everyone be prepared. We are going to amber alert now." Lights in the ship turned to an amber color and everyone prepared.

Caalin then gave the command, "Jump!" There was a flash then they were gone and reappeared near the blackhole they had jumped through before. The pirate ship was still in the area but did not detect the Seeker which made Caalin very happy that Mouse's new addition was working perfectly. He gave Ssam the command, "Move us away from here slowly then program our next jump back to Alliance Headquarters." He then told the others "Stay alert on the guns just in case." Once they had moved about 200 kilometers away from the pirate ship Caalin told Ssam to jump and again they were gone. Their next stop was the space near the Alliance Headquarters, Caalin radioed headquarters that the Seeker had completed its mission and was heading home with the information.

Mouse completed his physical and went back down to the shuttle bay to pull the information off the drones from the Raitora mission. Marty's crew had taken the containers out of the shuttle and placed them near the bulk head for him. After the scans were pulled he transferred the information to the main computer then went up to the bridge to go over it with Caalin before they docked at the Alliance Headquarters.

Once Mouse got to the bridge he followed Caalin and Dargon into the briefing room to look at the data. As they transferred the data to the map of the planet Caalin pointed to it, "There that's the Pirate base and it is a big one. Mouse once we dock I want you to transfer this data to the Alliance main computer." Mouse replied, "I have it ready to send the minute docking is complete."

Ssam brought the Seeker in slowly and the ground crew was there ready to lock the ship down as soon as he killed the engines. Before they were locked down and ready to leave the ship Caalin made an announcement over the ship's intercom, "I would like everyone to remain quite about the incident at Raitora and the loss of Mouse's arm, I am not asking you not to answer any questions should they come up, I am just asking you not to volunteer any information unless asked specifically. There are pirate spies everywhere and the less they know about us the better we can continue doing our jobs." He then turned to everyone on the bridge, "Ok let's go brief Alliance Councilman Moreland on our missions completion, Dargon you have the bridge should we need anything." Dargon replied, "I take it you may need a demonstration of Mouse's new invention." Caalin just nodded, "I will let you know."

As they left the ship the Councilman's secretary was there to greet them, "Welcome Captain Matthews the Councilman is waiting for you in conference room twelve if you will follow me." They entered the conference room and there was the Councilman setting at the end of the table looking at some reports, he looked up as the group walked in, "Welcome back Captain Matthews, I hope everyone on your ship are doing fine." He handed the reports he had to his secretary and told her what to do about them and Caalin and his team took their seats. Caalin turn to the Councilman, "My entire crew is doing fine sir and we are ready to give you a report on what we found in the Eridani Nebula." He continued, "We have transferred all the data over to the Alliance main computer for your convenience."

# CHAPTER 15

||||||||||||||||||||||||||||||||||||||||||

# THE BRIEFING AND
# PASSING OF TECHNOLOGY

Caalin brought the map of Raitora up and rotated it to show where the pirate base was located, "As you can see Councilman this base is a huge one and I estimate that there are at least one hundred ships there, but they are all medium and small with about twenty fighters." He then informed the councilman, "We did find people living on Kritilia but they were not part of the pirate clans and they were scattered all over the planet in small villages with no technology located on the planet at all."

Councilman Moreland looked at the map and the notes he had, "OK we will send the fifth fleet to engage those pirates, they are the closes ones to the nebula and I will also send the third fleet to back them up I think that will be enough Alliance ships to deal with them." He then looked at Caalin, "Your crew did an excellent job is there anything else you want to talk about?" Caalin looked over at Mouse and nodded his head, Mouse stood up, "Yes councilman I have a schematic of a generator that I designed and I think you will be excited to see it." Councilman Moreland smiled, "Well lieutenant Valtor I will be happy to look at it."

Mouse brought the schematic up as a hologram and pointed to the generator, "Councilman Moreland you are looking at the first stealth generator, it connects into the force shield generator and the two of them work together to bend light around the ship making it totally invisible." The Councilman looked shocked, "Are you telling me that this little generator can do that same thing that took scientist year to do on the Spirit?" Mouse smiled, "Yes sir, and I know that your science team has not been able to replicate the Spirit's stealth technology." Councilman Moreland scratched his head, "Can you prove that this works, the Alliance Council will want you to prove it before they will believe me."

This is where Caalin jumped back into the conversation, "Yes we can Councilman Moreland you see Mouse installed one on the Seeker and if you want proof just follow me." The Councilman stood up, "OK lead the way I want to see this thing work before I present it to the council." Caalin smiled, "Follow me and we will demonstrate the Valtor Stealth Generator."

As they were making their way out to the docking port Caalin radioed ahead, "Dargon take the Seeker just outside of the docking port and be prepared to go stealth on my command." Dargon replied, "Will do, this must be the demonstration I thought we would have to do." Caalin came back with, "Well Councilman Moreland wanted proof so let's give it to hm."

The Seeker moved away from the docking port, and then set waiting for Caalin's command. Caalin's team brought the Councilman outside on an observation deck so he could see the Seeker hovering above them. He turned to the Councilman, "See Councilman Moreland there is the Seeker in all her glory." Councilman Moreland looked up, "Yes I can see her clearly, and you've taken good care of her." Caalin smiled, "Ok

Dargon let's show the councilman what is new for the Seeker." Dargon laughed, "You got it boss; we are going invisible."

As the Councilman was staring at the Seeker all of a sudden it vanished from his sight. Caalin turned to the Councilman, "Check with the surveillance personnel to see if they are picking up the Seeker anywhere." The Councilman had his aid contact the surveillance tower to see if they had the Seeker still showing on their systems. The tower came back that they had the Seeker there a minute ago but now it is completely gone they are not picking up any trace of it on any of their systems.

Caalin contacted Dargon, "Ok you can shut it down and bring the ship back into the port." The Seeker then reappeared and slowly made its way back into the docking port. The tower reported back to the councilman that the Seeker just all of a sudden reappeared on their system. Councilman Moreland looked at Caalin, "Well son you have convinced me that the system works, but I will need to borrow your Engineer Officer for a couple of days to present it to our engineer team since it is his invention."

The Councilman thought for a moment then turned to Mouse, "We will have to register it as your invention so the Alliance will have to pay you for the rights to use it. Now the name Valtor Stealth Generator, why don't we call it the VSG for short, that way we can keep track on different versions by using number after the letter listing the one on the Seeker is the VSG-1 for first generation of the system." Mouse looked at the Councilman, "I am alright with that, it would be too long a name the other way."

Councilman Moreland then turned back to Caalin, "You and your crew take four days off while the young lieutenant is working with our engineering team. When your break is over we will have a new mission for you." Mouse whined, "I don't get the time off like everyone else?" Councilman Moreland laughed, "It depends on how fast you get our engineering team up to your level on your invention. Once they are able to build it you can join the rest of your crew, now come with me young man and I will introduce you to the team."

As the councilman and Mouse were walking away Caalin shouted to Mouse, "Let us know if you need anything and I will get it to you." Mouse waved his hand, "Thanks I will let you know." As Caalin and the others were making their way back to the ship one of the ground crew members asked him if there was anything that they could do for him. Caalin thought for a moment, "We do have two damage shuttles on board, if your team could see to their repair we would appreciate it, you see my engineering office is going to be busy for a while and the crew has been given time off." The crewman smiled, "No problem sir we will be happy to do it, I will send a crew over to pick them up and take them to the repair bay." Caalin thanked him and they continued on to the Seeker.

Once back on board Caalin made the announcement that everyone had four days off to do with as they wished, but if they were working on something that they needed to complete the work before leaving the ship should they do so.

Caalin looked over at Dargon, "What are you planning to do with your time off?" Dargon replied, "That's easy I plan to spend some time with Mari we haven't had any real time together since we came on board so we are overdue." Caalin laughed, "I know what you mean, I need to spend some time with Ang, but I think I need to stay close to the ship just in case I'm needed." Dargon put his hand on Caalin's shoulder,

"There are a lot of great restaurants and sites not far from here so don't think you have to stay on the ship the entire time." Caalin nodded, "Your right, we do need a little time off the ship and I know Ang would appreciate it."

Caalin then said, "I need to go down to the shuttle bay the ground crew is coming over to pick up the two damaged shuttles and take them for repairs and I want to be there incase they have any questions." Dargon replied, "Why don't I go with you." The two of them the left the bridge still talking about things to do near the Alliance Headquarters.

As the two of them were making their way down to the shuttle bay Caalin made a stop by the medical facility to see Ang. Ang smiled at him, "What brings you by, are you feeling ill?" Caalin just smiled at her, "When you are done here why don't you get cleaned up and change into something nice we are going out to dinner together just the two of us." Ang's eyes got wide, "Are you saying we are going on a date?" Caalin chuckled, "Yes I am, it has been to long since we had a proper date; so are you ok with that." Ang grabbed him and hugged him tight, "You know I am."

Caalin turned to leave but looked back, "Can you be ready in two hours; I have some business in the shuttle bay before I can get cleaned up." Ang blew him a kiss, "I will be ready and waiting." He then made his way out and made one more stop before getting to the Shuttle bay, it was engineering. Gahe was the only one in engineering finishing up a few things when Caalin walked up. Gahe turn to greet him, "What brings you by Caalin?" Caalin then told Gahe that he stopped by the medical facility and asked Ang out on a date, then advised Gahe that he might want to stop by and talk to Ssophia about maybe doing something with her. Gahe laughed, "Oh yeah, I know that Ang has already told Ssophia about your date by now so I will get straight there once I am done here; thanks for the heads up."

Finally Caalin made it to the shuttle bay just as the ground crew made it with a shuttle lift. The crewman told Caalin, "We brought our shuttle lift because we did not know if they were able to move on their own." Caalin pointed to the larger shuttle, "That one you will need the lift it took damage to the engine compartment, but the other one just took damage to the side when we slide the big one into it." The crewman replied, "Thanks we can take care of it from here we should have them ready in about two days so enjoy your free time." With that taken care of Caalin made his way to his room to get ready for his date with Ang.

# CHAPTER 16

‖‖‖‖‖‖‖‖‖‖‖‖‖‖‖‖‖‖‖‖‖‖‖‖‖‖‖‖‖‖‖‖

# FREE TIME

Caalin quickly showered and got dressed, he had on dark blue slacks, a light blue shirt and a medium blue blazer. He quickly brushed his hair and then gave himself thumbs up in the mirror before heading to Ang's room to pick her up. He stood outside of her room and pushed the button to let her know he was there, then heard her through the door, "I will be there in one minute." Caalin stood there patiently rocking back and forth on his heels when finally the door opened.

Caalin gasped, "You look beautiful." Ang was wearing a light blue dress that dropped just below her knees and on her left wrist was the bracelet he had given her when he asked her to be his girlfriend. She smiled at Caalin, "Well shall we head out, and I can't wait to see what is outside the docking port." Caalin took her hand, "Well let's head out and see what is out there."

Once they were off the ship they were met by a ground crewman with a cart, "Lieutenant Drake said you might need a ride to the main gate." Caalin nodded his head, "That would be wonderful, thank you." As he was helping Ang to her seat he whispered, "Remind me to thank Dargon later for arranging this, it could have been a long walk." Ang whispered back to him, "Or it could have been a short flight, or did you forget we both can fly." Caalin smiled and then looked down at her legs, "I don't think that would have been appropriate since you are wearing a dress." Ang blushed, "Oh, I didn't think about that, you're right, but just this time don't let that go to your head." The two of them laughed as the crewman drove them toward the main gate and the city beyond.

Once they reached the main gate a land cruiser was there to pick them up and take them into the city. The driver walked around to greet them and introduce herself, "I am Liana and I will be your driver for your trip into the city, Lieutenant Drake arranged for me to take you to the restaurant Lunam Amantes unless you prefer somewhere else." Caalin looked over at Ang, "Does that sound ok to you?" Ang smiled, "If Dargon recommends it then I am fine with it; as long as I am with you it doesn't matter where we go." Caalin turned back to Liana, "Restaurant Lunam Amantes it is then."

Liana drove them through the city, passing stores, restaurants and apartment complexes then up the side of a mountain on the other side of the city. On the back side of the mountain set the restaurant on the edge of a cliff overlooking a beautiful waterfall running down into a large lake below. Liana stopped the cruiser in front of the entrance and went around opening the door for her passengers. As Ang stepped out she looked around and smiled, "This is a beautiful place." Liana gave Caalin a small device, "When you are ready to go just press that button and I will be here within minutes to pick you up." Caalin thanked her as he and Ang turned to go inside the restaurant.

As the two of them walked up to the hostess she asked for their name so Caalin replied, "Caalin Matthews and Angiliana Avora." The hostess jumped with surprise, "Yes Captain Matthews we have your table waiting for you please follow me." She led them through the restaurant out onto the terrace and set them at a secluded table overlooking the waterfall and lake. As they were taking their seats Ang asked, "How did she know you were a Captain?" Caalin replied, "Dargon must have told them."

The waiter soon appeared, "Captain Matthews may I take your order?" Caalin paused for a minute, "I have a quick question how does everyone here know that I am a captain; did Lieutenant Drake mention it when he set up our reservation?" The Waiter shook his head, "No sir everyone here knows about the youngest captain ever to be given his own ship. You are the person, who finally won the on winnable battle that drove all the Military Academy students crazy, plus our owner is from Averiaera and we also know you are the Hero of Dorrye."

Caalin lowered his head, "We are ready to order now." The waiter took their order and before he left asked if it would be ok for the owner to stop by their table later to meet him. Caalin told him it would be ok as long as he did not make a big deal of it in front of the other guest. The waiter nodded, "Thank you sir, I will let him know." As the waiter walked of Ang laughed, "You are slowly becoming a legion and I don't know if I am worthy of being by your side." Caalin looked at her, "Stop that, I am no legion and you are the only one I want by my side." Ang smirked, "Oh just me, what about the rest of our friends?" Caalin lowered his head, "You know what I meant." Ang laughed, "I'm sorry I couldn't help myself you are so cute when you are flustered, and yes I know what you meant."

Soon the meal arrived and the two of them set enjoying the food and talking about the stars, the water fall and the moon reflecting off the waters of the lake. After they had finished the meal and the desert that came after it the owner made his appearance at their table.

He introduced himself, "I am Damirin Liene the owner of Lunam Amantes and I welcome you Hero of Dorrye." Caalin quickly spoke up, "Please stop with the hero talk, I am no hero I just did what I could at that time." Damirin came back with, "I am sorry but you are a hero, especially to those whose lives you saved and everyone related to them, my parents live in Dorrye and they were saved by your great feat, so sir to those people and myself you will always be a hero."

After hearing this Ang finally stepped into the conversation, "Damirin, Caalin is a humble individual, he doesn't like to be called hero for doing things he is capable of doing or for doing things he thinks is right. He did what he did because he could do it not to be a hero, so if you could please just call him Caalin or Captain Matthews." Damirin backed up and lowered his head, "As you wish Princess Angiliana, I will honor your request." This sent a chill down Ang's back, "Damirin please stop with the princess too." Again Damirin replied, "As you wish." Caalin got a good chuckle out of Ang's reaction and she elbowed him in the side for it.

Damirin then asked, "Caalin would the two of you mind stepping into my office and having a picture made with me I would love to have one for my office wall?" Caalin looked over to Ang, "If it is ok with Ang then I am ok with it." Ang said yes and Damirin smiled, "Thank you and don't worry about your meal it is on me." He led them to his office where he had his secretary take the picture and within minutes had two prints of it, one large one and one medium. In the picture Caalin stood between Ang and Damirin and the two of them had their wings fluffed out so it looked like they were standing in front of a feathered wall. Caalin press the button on the device Liana had given him then he and Ang signed both of the pictures for Damirin and he then escorted them back out to the front of the restaurant and their waiting cruiser.

Liana asked, "Where would the two of you like to go now?" Caalin looked over at Ang and could see she was tired, "I think we should head back it has been a long day for us, but if you are available tomorrow would you mind taking Ang and her friends around for a shopping day?" Liana perked up, "I would love too; in fact I know a lot of great shops to take them." She then gave Caalin a card, "Have someone contact this number and tell them you have requested Liana for the shopping trip, I will make the arrangements when I get back to the office." She pulled up to the main gate, "I am sorry this is as far as I am allowed to go but there should be a cart there to take you were ever you need to go on the base." Caalin thanked her for the evening and said they would call her for tomorrow but he wasn't sure for what time. She waved as she drove off, "No problem I will be waiting to hear from you."

Ang and Caalin showed their IDs to the guard at the gate and he had a crewman with a cart drive them back to the ship. As they were walking back on board Ang asked, "Why did you set up the shopping trip for tomorrow?" Caalin laughed, "I know you, Ssophia and the other girls love to shop, and I have some things to take care of like checking on Mouse and I didn't want you to get bored setting around the ship." They stepped onto the ship and Ang pulled Caalin into a dark corner just inside the door, then gave him a kiss that he would remember. She then whispered into his ear, "You are one thoughtful boyfriend, don't you every change." He then walked her back to her room, gave her another kiss and told her good night before heading to his own room.

A few minutes after she got to her room there was a ring at her door and when Ang opened it Ssophia was standing there smiling. Ang invited her in and the two of them discussed what they had done that evening. Ssophia told Ang about Gahe taking her to this quaint little café in the middle of the city and the wonderful meal they had. Ang told her about the restaurant Caalin had taken her to and that he had set it up for their driver to take all the girls shopping the next day. The two of them continued talking late into the night until they both could barely keep their eyes open and Ssophia left to go back to her room.

# CHAPTER 17

||||||||||||||||||||||||||||||||||||||||||

# DAY TWO OF TIME OFF

The next morning Caalin, Dargon and Jason were having breakfast together when the girls came into the dining hall. Caalin looked up and there were Ang, Ssophia, Sisten, Marjori, Jean, Mari, Patrish, Clair and even Faelara and Resrassira. Caalin asked, "Are all of you going shopping together, and if so where are the other girls?" Ang answers, "These are the only ones that wanted to shop Atira, Evalon, Tealana, Keyan, Asgaya and Astra are going to join us later for lunch at Café Deltor." She continued, "We asked Tehaena and the other girls in the kitchen to join us but they are heading to the open market in the plaza to see if they can get some sea food."

Caalin just shook his head, "I had better let Liana know how many of you there are so she can make sure she has a big enough vehicle." Ang smiled at him, "Thank you, you're the best." Ssophia turn to Caalin "Let her know we will be ready in about an hour, we want to eat first shopping takes a lot of energy." Caalin laughed, "The way you girls shop I tend to agree with you."

Caalin then turn to Dargon and Jason, "I am going to check up on Mouse this morning do you two want to join me?" Jason replied, "I'm sorry Ssam and I promised Gahe and Jon we would help them run some test on the system so we are needed on the bridge for that, Ssam is already there now." Dargon then told him, "I am going to visit my grandfather he is back on base for a few days and we have some catching up to do." Caalin just sighed, "I would check with Marty and his team but I know they are moving equipment around and picking up supplies."

He finished his breakfast and made his way to one of the offices on the docking port to contact Liana and inform her of the number of people Ang was bringing with her. Liana laughed, "No problem Captain Matthews I will bring a vehicle large enough for them all." Caalin replied, "Thank you for understanding and would you please just call me Caalin from now on there is no need to be so formal." Liana laughed again, "I will remember that Caalin."

After the call He made his way toward the engineering complex to check on Mouse, and as he was walking one of the crewmen stopped on a cart to see if he would like a ride. Caalin told him, "Thanks but I prefer to walk, that way I get to see more of the base and talk to people that I meet along the way." The crewman nodded, "Ok sir but if you need a ride anywhere just let us know." Caalin thought for a moment, "Well there are ten women from my crew heading into the city in about thirty minutes, could you arrange transportation for them from the Seeker to the front gate; I have someone picking them up there." The crewman nodded, "That will not be a problem I will take care of it now, have a great day sir." Caalin waved as the cart pulled away heading in the direction of the Seeker while the crewman was radioing to arranging more transportation to meet him at the ship.

Forty minutes later Caalin arrived at the Engineering Complex and was met at the entrance by one of the receptionist, "Could I help you sir?" Caalin gave her a smile, "I'm Captain Matthews of the AS1-Seeker and I am here to see my Engineering Officer Lieutenant Valtor." The receptionist perked up, "Captain Matthews it is nice to meet you I have heard so much about you." She stood up and motioned, "If you will follow me sir I will take you to the Lieutenant." Caalin followed her down the hall until they reached a large set of double doors, "You will find Lieutenant Valtor in this hanger."

Caalin walked through the doors and looked around and there was Mouse leaning into what looked like large engine housing. He walked over and cleared his throat, "Are you planning to crawl inside to hide from everyone?" Mouse jumped, "Oh it's you, no I was just checking to make sure they had the locations drilled properly for the azerithium crystals; this is going to be the stealth generator for a large command cruiser." Caalin looked at the size of the housing, "Does it have to be that big for a larger cruiser?" Mouse replied, "Yes it does, it has to match the output of the shield generator so it has to be that big. This one is VSG-4; it is the 4th generation of the system. VSG-1 was the first size I made that is in the Seeker, but we have created a smaller version VSG-2 for the shuttles and fighters, as well as a medium version VSG-3 for the mid size cruisers and battle ships."

Caalin looked around the room and could see other engineers working on engine housings of their own. He then turned back to Mouse, "Well it looks like you have been one busy individual." Mouse wiped his forehead, "Yes it has been busy but I will be done with my part of the work by tomorrow around lunch, then I hand it over to the Engineers here to do the rest." Caalin smiled at Mouse, "Great why don't I come by tomorrow and pick you up for lunch in the city, my treat." Mouse slapped Caalin on the shoulder, "You're on, and I will be waiting with my appetite." Caalin turned to leave, "OK I will bring Ang and Sisten with me so be ready."

Caalin left and made his way back to the ship and once back on board made his way to the bridge to check on Ssam and Jason. As he walked in he asked, "How is everything going with your test?" Ssam replied, "We just wrapped them up and everything is working great." Caalin smiled, "That's good, I just got back from checking in with Mouse and he should be back on board tomorrow afternoon, I am planning to take Ang and Sisten over to pick him up and take him to lunch to celebrate his achievement." Ssam laughed, "That is good, I was thinking about taking Clair out to lunch tomorrow too, I hope they get all their shopping out of their systems by then."

The three of them were laughing when a call from Marty came through, "Caalin could you come down to the shuttle bay, we just got our two shuttles back but we have four new ships that they are assigning to the Seeker." Caalin replied back, "I will be right down." Ssam looked over at Jason then back to Caalin, "Do you mind if we join you I want to see what they are assigning us." Caalin just nodded his head, "Come ahead, the more the merrier."

The three of them made it to the shuttle bay and Marty was there to greet them. He turned to Caalin, "We have moved the two small shuttles over in the small corned on the starboard side and then lined the four large one over on the port wall, but I need to know where you would like me to put the four that are being loaded now." Caalin looked over at the bay door and saw a slick small one man fighter coming through the door; he could see the labeling on it that showed AS1-F1. Caalin looked around the bay, "These are small fighters; I think you could put two along the wall with the large shuttle and the other two in front of them."

Marty looked over at the area, "I think that will work, I will get them moved over there now." As the first fighter was moved into position Caalin had time to walk over and take a good look at the ship. It was a sleek fighter with two laser cannons that popped out of the starboard and port side and rotated up and down between sixty degrees and three hundred degrees, the rear wing that started at the bottom of the fighter and circled up and over the back about two meters had a laser cannon that popped out of the top and rotated not only three hundred and sixty degree around and move up and down. Caalin looked over at the others, "I wander if Mouse could put stealth generators on these babies." Ssam looked at the fighter, "Knowing Mouse he will have them installed before we ever get to fly one."

# CHAPTER 18

|||||||||||||||||||||||||||||||||||||||||||||

# ARRIVAL OF NEW SHIPS

After all the fighters had been loaded onboard the ship Caalin looked at the others, "Well it looks like it is time for me to make a visit to Councilman Moreland; I need to see what the plan is for the fighters." Caalin left the ship and made his way to the councilman office where the receptionist informed him that she had been expecting him to show up. Caalin looked bewildered and she smiled, "You received the new fighters today and Councilman Moreland said you would probably be showing up to find out why." Caalin nodded his head, "Well he was right about that."

The receptionist laughed, "Well the Councilman is not here today but he gave me the information to pass on to you. The day after tomorrow you and whom every you decide you want to be able to fly those fighter will go through a training course on them. What I need from you is a list of names of all the personnel that you want to go through the training and I don't want to rush you but I need the list by noon tomorrow to arrange the training ships." Caalin looked at her, "OK let me get this straight, I have four fighters but I can have as many of my people trained to fly them as I want?" The receptionist nodded, "That is correct, you never know when you will need someone else to man one of them." Caalin turned to leave, "You will have my list as soon as I can get it to you." She waved, "I will be here waiting Captain Matthews, pick you fighter pilots well."

Caalin made his way back to the ship and as he was boarding Dargon walked up and asked what has been going on while he was gone. Caalin went into detail about getting the fighters and talking with the receptionist and as soon as he finished his update Dargon smiled, "I want to be on the top of the list for the training." Caalin just looked at him, "Your name will be right below mine." Dargon just laughed, "I had no doubt that your name would be first, but whom else are we going to pick." Caalin thought for a moment, "Well we need to wait for everyone to get back onboard tonight then I will call a meeting, and since it will be the entire crew we might need to have it in the dining hall to have the room for them all."

Everyone began returning to the ship later that afternoon and once Caalin got the report that all hands were back on board he made the announcement that he wanted everyone to meet in the dining hall at 17:00 for a ship meeting. It was 16:00 and the girls had stored away all the things they had purchase during their shopping trip and Ssophia, Ang and Sisten were in the medical facility bringing everything back on line, Gahe had asked them to shut everything down during his repairs to prevent any surges or back feed through the system. The three of them were wondering why Caalin called for a meeting of the entire crew, normally it was with the officers and they passed the information down to the rest of the crew.

Soon it was 17:00 and everyone was gathered in the dining hall waiting on Caalin to let them know what was going on. Caalin stepped up on a chair so everyone could see and hear him, "Everyone I don't know if you are aware or not but today we took delivery of four single pilot fighter ships." He paused then continued, "I have been informed that the Alliance is going to train our pilots for these ships, but I need to give them a list of the people that will be going through the training." Clair asked, "Since there are four fighters are we only training four people?" Caalin smiled, "I am glad you asked that, no we can have them train as many people as we want, it never hurts to have more people trained to fly them, because you never know when we need a replacement pilot." Everyone started mumbling and Caalin cleared his throat to get their attention, "What I need to know is how many of you are interested in learning to fly them and willing to use them if we need them in a combat situation." He could see a little concern in some of their eyes, "I only want volunteers, no one will be force to go through the training that does not want to fly one and possibly have to fight in one. If you want to be on the list please send me your name by 23:00 tonight as I need to turn the list over to the Alliance office by noon tomorrow."

After the meeting he dismissed everyone and headed back to the bridge and was followed by Clair and Jason whom he already knew that they would be some of the first to want the training. Once they were on the bridge Caalin turned to them both, "I already know and have your names on the list right below mine and Dargon's." No sooner had he said that Ssam and Ric walked in and Ssam said, "That's good you have two more to add to the list with Ric and myself." Caalin replied, "That's great at least we have six people for the training but I did set a dead line so hopefully we will have more."

Later Caalin made his way back to the dining hall to meet Ang for dinner and as he set down he asked, "Well are you not volunteering for the fighter training?" Ang laughed, "Are you kidding, someone has to be around to patch all you crazy pilots up when you slam a hatch on your fingers." Caalin laughed, "You're right we can be clumsy, besides I feel better with you here to help with the injured should there be any." Ssophia walked up and over heard the conversation, "That won't stop her from worrying about you, for some reason you seem to attract injuries." Caalin just replied, "Well someone has to give you work to do."

The three of them were laughing when Rostrik and Faelara walked over to their table. Rostrik looked over at Caalin, "Captain Matthews the two of us would like to be considered for the pilot training if you will have us." Caalin look up at Rostrik, "First drop the Captain Matthews it is just Caalin, and I will be happy to add you to the list why would you think I wouldn't?" Faelara spoke, "You see sir our race has been shunned as pilots; they tell us all we are good for is ground assault and nothing else." Caalin gave the two of them a stern look, "Well I am not they whomever they might be and on my ship you will be treated the same as the rest of the crew. If you want to pilot a fighter or any other one of the space craft on board I will make sure you get the training you need." They both thanked Caalin for his kind words and stated they both wanted to be included in the training on the fighters.

Later that night Caalin's deadline passed and he only had eight volunteers for the training so he added all the names to his list to send over to the Councilman's office and the list read Caalin Matthews, Dargon Drake, Clair Tilone, Jason Rogers, Ric Harset, Ssamuel Ssallazz, Rostrik Olhill, and Faelara Ashalwelia. Caalin smiled at the list, "That gives me two different teams for the fighters so we can work in shifts if we need to." With that complete he sent the list and got ready for bed.

# CHAPTER 19

|||||||||||||||||||||||||||||||||||||||||||||

# MOUSE'S RETURN
# TO THE SEEKER

The next morning Caalin got up early and went to breakfast, while he was eating his meal Belrion came over to talk with him, "Well Caalin did you get very many volunteers for your fighter training?" Caalin smiled, "I got more than I thought I would, I figured everyone were in positions they were comfortable in and did not want to make any changes. I pretty much knew who I would get as volunteers but I was really surprises when Rostrik and Faelara asked to be added to the list."

Belrion replied, "I am surprised they even volunteered since they are Virerian and most races look down on them, I am glad that everyone on this ship treats them like anyone else. Their race was almost wiped out by the pirates and although they are great fighter they are looked at like they are only good for cannon folder and that's truly a shame." Caalin looked at Belrion, "Well that is not the crew of the Seeker, we all look at them as part of our family and anyone that thinks otherwise will have to deal with us." Belrion looked at Caalin before he walked away, "Thank you sir for how you treat your crew; I was right in volunteering to join your crew thanks to Princess Phanasian's recommendation and to be honest I would have volunteered for the fighter training, but my wife

Tehaena would have killed me before the training ever began." Caalin laughed, "You know I think you are right about that." Belrion walked away saying, "Enjoy your breakfast sir."

After breakfast Caalin made his way to the bridge where he was the only one there since they were in dock and did not need to man the systems. He set down in his seat and received a message from the Councilman's office that read, "*We received your list for pilot training and the training will begin at 08:00 tomorrow, please report to docking port twenty seven by that time.*" Caalin then sent the information to everyone on the list and asked them to meet him for breakfast at 05:30 the next morning and they would go to the fighter training docking port together."

After setting on the bridge alone for almost an hour he decided to make his way down to the shuttle bay to look at the fighters again. Once there he walked over and open the hatch, and then crawled into the fighter looking at all the controls. There were switches on the left side that controlled opening the cannons and on the right side there were controls for the thrusters, shields, and empty switches for any other systems that they needed to add later. He smiled as he thought to himself, that's where Mouse can add the stealth generator. He looked at the yoke for steering the ship, it was an elongated U shape that you push forward to descend, pull back to ascend and turn left or right to go in those direction, but along the sides of the yoke were the buttons for the laser guided cannons. There was one on the top of both sides of the U shape for the left and right cannons and a trigger like switch on the front of the right side for the top cannon.

Caalin had been in the fighter most of the morning when Marion came over, "Are you aware of what time it is, Angiliana has been trying to locate you for the last fifteen minutes." Caalin jumped out of the fighter,

"No I total forgot what time it was thanks for informing me." He then left the shuttle bay and made his way back to the bridge where Ang and Sisten were waiting on him. Caalin quickly apologized for being late and Ang just looked at him, "You were in the shuttle bay playing with your new toys weren't you?" Caalin just lowered his head, "Yes and I am so sorry I am late."

The girls finally told him they forgave him and they made their way off the ship and down to the docking port where Ang had already arranged for someone to take them to the Engineering Complex to meet Mouse. When they arrived they found Mouse in the hanger telling everyone goodbye and that they had the schematics so they would be able to complete the building and installation on their own. As the four of them were leaving Sisten asked, "What was the hardest part of working on those engines?" Mouse looked over at her, "It was determining the number of crystals each engine version required to work properly but after a while we came up with a formula that worked."

While they made their way out to get their ride to the main gate Mouse asked, "What is going on over at the Seeker?" Caalin went into detail about the new fighters they received and who was picked for the pilot training then Mouse looked at him, "Did you add my name to the list?" Caalin looked straight into his eyes, "No I did not, I need you on the Seeker someone has to be able to handle every engineering issue that comes up and I don't know anyone I trust more that you." He paused for a moment, "And besides Sisten would have killed me had I added your name to that list." Sisten gave a little smirk, "You are darn right I would have." Everyone broke into laughter as they reached the main gate.

At the main gate Liana was waiting on them to take them to Café Deltor so they all piled into the land cruiser and off they went. On the way to the café Caalin introduced Liana to Mouse then told Mouse that she was the best driver on the planet, if you know what you wanted she knows where to take you. That is when Ang and Sisten both said they got to know liana a lot better since she joined them in their shopping extravaganza. Liana laughed, "Yeah and I am going to have to work some extra shifts to make up for the credits I spent."

Soon they were at the café enjoying their meal as Mouse was filling them in on all the test they had ran on the new stealth engines he created. After the meal Liana was there to pick them up and drop them at the main gate where a crewman was there to drive them back to the ship. As they boarded the ship Mouse looked over to Caalin, "I want to see the new fighters so I will know what I have to work with." Caalin told Ang he would see her later and Mouse quickly gave Sisten a kiss and told her the same, then the two of them made their way down to the shuttle bay.

As they entered the shuttle bay Mouse could see the ships, he turned to Caalin, "These are the newest models and they are suppose to be the fastest ones the Alliance has, what did you do to get them?" Caalin scratched his head, "Absolutely nothing, they just brought them to us." Mouse turned back to the ships, "I wonder what the Councilman has in store for us on our next mission." Caalin replied, "We will worry about that when it comes up, my question to you is do you think you can install a stealth generator on them?" Mouse thought for a moment, "Let me get the schematics for the ship from the Engineering Complex main computer and look it over, I should have an answer for you by tomorrow morning." Caalin put his hand on Mouse's back, "Go for it my friend, if we get caught up in a fight I want every advantage we can have."

Mouse turned and started out of the shuttle bay, "Well if I am going to do this I need to start the research now." Caalin smiled, "Well if you need anything from me just let me know and I will see what strings I can pull." Mouse left heading to his quarters and Caalin made his way back up to the bridge.

# CHAPTER 20

||||||||||||||||||||||||||||||||||||||||||

# MOUSE AND THE FIGHTERS

Later on that evening Caalin walked into the dining hall to meet Ang, Ssophia and Gahe for dinner as he entered Mouse flagged him over to the table where He and Sisten were sitting. He looked up at Caalin, "I did all the calculations and I can have stealth generators on the fighter by noon the day after tomorrow." Caalin slapped him on the shoulder, "That is great, get started on them as soon as you can." Mouse smiled, "Consider it done." Caalin then left to join his dinner companions.

Caalin was enjoying his meal when Ang asked, "Do you have time tomorrow to go into the city with me; I saw this lovely necklace yesterday that I would love to get and send to Betsy, her birthday is coming up in a week." Caalin smiled at her, "If it is for you and Betsy I would be happy to accompany you, but I will not be able to go until 10:00 if that is ok, we can grab lunch in the city." Ang replied, "That would be find, I always enjoy having lunch with you."

Gahe asked, "Why do you have to wait until 10:00 to leave?" Caalin answered, "I want to go over to Councilman Moreland's office and talk to his staff about the fighter training and the people that will be attending it. I just want to get more details that his receptionist did not have before." Ssophia spoke up, "I hear you have eight people total.'

Caalin said, "Yes I have eight people signed up for the training." Ssophia came back with, "I am glad Gahe did not volunteer for it, I would worry about him too much." Gahe jumped, "You need not have worried at all I know my limits and piloting a space craft is not among my capabilities, I tend to get nauseated trying to watch the controls and what is going on around me, I'm better off working on them instead." Caalin laughed, "I understand I had some friends back home that were the same way, you could not get them anywhere near the pilot's seat." The four of them continued talking and eating until dinner was over and Caalin walked Ang back to her room.

After dropping Ang off at her room he made his way down to the shuttle bay to look at the fighters again before going to bed thinking that may give him some more questions to ask. He walked into the shuttle bay and immediately saw Mouse, who had already opened the engine compartment on one of the fighters and was head first in it up to his waist. Caalin walked over and slapped the side of the compartment with his hand making Mouse jump and bang his head. Mouse shouted, "Who did that you scared me half to death." Caalin laughed, "It would not have scared you at all if you had not dove in to the engine compartment head first." Mouse then shouted, "Caalin I should smack you for that, but I won't I need you to help me get out of here I think I am stuck." Caalin laughed the entire time he was pulling Mouse out of the engine compartment and then said, "You didn't have to get started on them tonight." Mouse replied, "I just wanted to see how much room I had inside to work with, that will determent the configuration of the generator I put in them." Caalin looked over into the compartment, "It doesn't look like there is a lot of room in there; are you sure you are going to be able to do it?" Mouse gave Caalin a look of disappointment, "You do know who you are talking to don't you; if I can't make it work I should just give up on engineering."

Caalin laughed, "We don't need you doing that, I need my number one engineer around." Mouse close the compartment back down and secured it, "Well I have all the information I need and will get started on them first thing tomorrow." Caalin slapped him on the shoulder, "Great pal, now let go get some sleep we both have a busy day tomorrow." The two of them walked by the charging stations for the androids as Mouse looked over at them, "I think I may have one of those droids help me with my work tomorrow." Caalin replied, "Use as many of them you need Marty's team doesn't seem to be able to keep them busy right now."

The next morning Caalin was up early and went to the bridge to see if there was anything that needed his attention, but no one was on the bridge so he made his way to the dining hall for breakfast. As he walked in Mouse was on his way out, "Well Caalin I see I am not the only one up this early, I'm heading down to get started on the fighters, and I will give you an update on them this evening." Caalin just waved at him, "Take your time and don't over work yourself." Mouse shouted back, "Don't worry about that I am going to use a couple of those droids to help, I may even drag Ssam and Gahe down there too." Caalin laughed, "Good luck with getting those two down there, but if you're able to you may want to grab Dargon as well."

After breakfast Caalin made his way off ship and down to the councilman's office and as he enter the receptionist looked up, "Captain Matthews nice to see you again today, what brings you in this early in the morning." Caalin replied, "First I wanted to make sure you received the list of personnel who volunteered for fighter training, and I also was hoping you could give me more information about it." She

117

leaned over and picked up a sheet of paper, "I have the list of all eight people right here and I have sent a copy of it to the instructor in charge of the training. You and your crew need to be a docking port twenty seven by 08:00 tomorrow morning, you will then be transported to the Alliance Training Cruiser Gevechts for your training." She then put the list down, "I am sorry but that is all the information I have that I can share with you." Caalin gave her a smile, "Thank you very much that is more information than I had before." He then turned and left the office heading back to the ship, then he remembered he was taking Ang into the city so he stopped and contacted Liana to pick them up at the main gate.

Caalin meet Ang in the medical facility just before 10:00, "Well my lady are you ready to depart for the city, I have Liana picking us up at the main gate." Ang quickly said yes then turn an told Ssophia and Sisten she would see them later. Caalin took her hand and the two of them made their way off the ship where a crewman was waiting to drive them to the main gate. Once they reached the gate Liana was there waiting on them to take them into the city.

As they walked up Liana smiled, "You two make the cutest couple, where would you like me to take you this morning." Ang looked at her, "Do you remember the jewelry store we went to where I saw that charming necklace, we would like to stop there please, I need to pick up a birthday present and send it back home." Liana snapped to attention, "Your wish is my command." The three of them were laughing as they got into the vehicle and drove away.

When they reached the jewlry store Liana told them she would wait at the vehicle while they were inside she could not afford any more large purchases. Caalin laughed, "Ok thanks, we will not be long." Ang walked up to the man at the counter and he imediatly remembered her from the day before. "I see you are back today, is there something I can show you", he asked. Ang replied, "do you remember the necklace I was looking at yesterday, I have decided I want to purchase it please."

The man quickly opened the cabinet and pulled out the necklace and handed it to her to reexamine and as she was doing so he noticed the bracelet she was wearing. He then asked her, "Your bracelet is it made form Tiemmondine?"Ang looked over at Caalin, "I don't know what it is made of do you?" Caalin shook his head, "No all I know is it was made from a meteorite that fell into the sea and spent years on the bottom until it was brought up in a fishman's net."

He then asked Ang, "Do you wear the bracelet all the time?" Ang nodded, "Yes I always have it on." He smiled, "Then we can test it to see if it is Tiemmondine, you see Tiemmondine has a special ability." He then went over to a work table and picked up a magnet, "If you don't mine may I see your arm?" Ang helt out her arm with the bracelet and the clerk then helt the magnet up to the bracelet, "Now this is not a powerful magnet but it will do for this test." After a minute he placed the magnet up against a sheet of metal and it did not stick at all, he smiled, "It is Tiemmondine."

Caalin then asked, "Ok, so it drained the magnet of its magnatism." The Clerk smiled, "Yes but that is not all, since the young lady constantly wears it the stone more than likely has already synchronized with her body." He then pulled out a ring and tied a string to it, "Now young lady if you will just imagine a energy ring around the bracelet and I can show you what it can do." Ang agreed and staired at the bracelet imaging a field of energy encircling it. The clerk then lowered the ring toward the bracelet and to Ang and Caalin's surprise it stopped in the air a few inches above the bracelet.

Caalin looked at the Clerk, "What did we just see?" The clerk laughed, "You see Tiemmondine can take in and store magnetic energy and if a person has worn it long enough for it to synchronize to them they can use it to product a force field around the bracelet." Caalin scratched his head, "So it can only produce a force field big enough to protect itself." The clerk lowered his head, "Yes that is all, but it can store a thousand tmes more enegy but you would need a really big magnet to do it and I don't know where you would find one that big."

Ang looked at the clerk, "Thank you for the deminstration and letting us know what the bracelet is made of, but can I pay of the necklace now please?" The clerk jumped and quickly appologized for taking up their valuble time but that was the first time he had actually seen Tiemmondine. Ang paid for the necklace and the two of them made their way back out to meet Liana.

Back in the vehicle Liana asked, "Where would you like to go next." Caalin looked over to Ang and smiled, "Cafe Deltor and we would love for you to join us for lunch, you have been so kind to us since we arrive I would love to treat you to lunch." Before Liana could say anything Ang said, "And we will not take no as an answer." Liana smiled, "Well in that case I will be happy to join you."

The three of them enjoyed lunch together and afterwards Liana drove them back to the base and said she would see them later. Once back on board the ship Caalin kiss Ang and made his way to the shuttle bay to see how Mouse was making out with the stealth generators. As he walked up Mouse was securing the engine compartment of one of the fighters so he asked, "How are things going, I thought you were going to get Ssam, Gahe and Dargon to help with the work." Mouse stared straight at Caalin, "Those three were useless I got more work out of those two androids than I did either of them, so I ran them off." He looked around, "Well these three have been completed I just have the last one over there to do and they all will be ready for testing." Caalin replied, "Well the testing may have to wait until we are back in space, but you should be able to run simulations to verify them." Mouse lowered his head, "Well that will have to do for now, but as soon as we are away from here I want a good test." Caalin smiled, "You will get every test you want once we are away from here."

Caalin left Mouse to do his work and made his way back up to the bridge, he wanted to talk to his fighter team about the training. Once on the bridge he asked Astra to contact everyone on his fighter team list for a briefing. She contacted them all and when they were all assembled in the briefing room Caalin told them everything he found out. He then told them he would see them in the dining hall at 04:00 for breakfast and they would all go over to docking port twenty seven together, he then released them to do what they wanted. He made one more pass through the bridge then made his way to his room to get some rest before dinner.

# CHAPTER 21

||||||||||||||||||||||||||||||||||||||||||||||||

# FIGHTER TRAINING

Later at dinner Ang was telling Caalin that she plan to have the councilman's receptionist send the bracelet she bought to Betsy the next morning and then Marjori, Jean, Ssophia and herself were going to have Liana take them up to the Luman Amantes for lunch, but this time she was going to have Liana join them. Caalin touched her hand, "That's a great idea; Liana has been good to us while we were here and I consider her a good friend." Ang took his hand and squeezed it, "I do too, she is a very good friend and I will make sure she knows it."

After dinner Caalin made his rounds through the ship to see what was going on and to talk to everyone he ran across during his excursion. When he got to the shuttle bay Mouse was securing the last fighter and as Caalin walked up Mouse patted the ship, "Well this was the last one and it's all complete." Caalin looked at the fighter, "Great job, but don't you think you should go get something to eat, I think Sisten may be waiting on you." Mouse panicked, "Oh it's that late, I need to get cleaned up quickly and head right up, and if you see her let her know I will be there soon." Caalin laughed, "I will make sure she gets the message."

He then walked through the cargo hanger and it was all quite, nothing there but the androids Mouse had helping him recharging themselves. Then on his way to his room he walked by the medical facility and saw Sisten putting away some equipment so he stopped to give her Mouse's message. Sisten giggled, "Thank you for letting me know, but I thought that was where he was, he tends to get caught up in what he's doing." Caalin told her to have a good dinner and made his way to his room and a hot shower.

While in the shower Caalin got to thinking about what the clerk has said about Ang's bracelet being able to store magnetic energy. He then remembered that gravity is just the magnetic field that surrounds a planet so could he put that energy into the bracelet? Then he remembered what the Mystic Serane had said to him *"This bracelet is what you need to give the young lady you hold in your heart, and it will protect her in the future"* was that what she meant? He told himself that he needed to test the idea, but it would have to wait until after the fighter training.

The next morning he was in the dining hall at 04:00 and as soon as he walked in Faelara and Rostrik waved him over to the large table they had picked for everyone to eat together before heading off to training. Caalin asked, "Have the two of you been here long?" Faelara smiled, "We just got here ourselves so we were not waiting on you."

After a couple of minutes the others started showing up and it wasn't long they were all enjoying a great breakfast that Teroth and Nasth had prepared and Orianna had brought out to them. They all set, ate and talked until it was 05:30 and Caalin stood up, "Well we should all make our way down to meet our ride." He told Orianna thanks for the wonderful meal and to give the chefs his compliments. She waved, "I will sir and you all be safe out there."

The eight of them made their way off the ship and were met by a crewman with a cart large enough to transport all of them. They all took a seat and he drove them over to docking port twenty seven where a shuttle was waiting for them to take them to the Gevechts a trainer cruiser. Everyone boarder the shuttle and they were ferried off the planet and up to the cruiser.

Once onboard the Gevechts they were taken to a training room full of pods, there they met the instructor Admiral Kerin Escov. The Admiral looked over the group then to Caalin, "I see lad you have chosen two Virerians as part of your team are you sure about that?" Caalin looked him straight in the eyes, "Sir I am one hundred percent confident in all of my crew and they are no exception." The Admiral laughed, "No need to get mad lad, I was just testing your loyalty to those who server with you, unfortunately there are a lot of commanders, even in the Alliance, that don't think highly of Virerians, but I am glad to see that you are not one of those."

After hearing the Admiral, Rostrik had to speak up, "Sir if I may, Captain Matthews has done nothing but show us respect, he has gone as far as to tell us that we are part of his family as are every member of his crew, and if asked I would give my life for him." The Admiral looked back at Caalin, "Well lad it seems the stories I have heard about you are true, you do draw people that trust you to your side."

Admiral Escov then began his training, "These pods you see are the first phase of your training they are fighter simulators if each of you will pick one we will begin your training." Once everyone was in a pod the Admiral went to the control room and talked to them through the communications system. He announced, "These systems are to familiarize you with the controls and feel of the ships. Their function is exactly the same as on the fighters so get familiar with them. The first part of the training you will be flying information and in and out of cruisers to get use to moving around other shipped while fighting, and then we will step it up and add enemy fighter ships so you all need to familiarize yourselves with the weapon system. We will keep a tally of your performance and rate you by that from best to worst. Ok let's begin part one of your training."

The first part went on for over two hours before the systems came to a halt and the Admiral came out to talk with them, "Well I have to say everyone did a lot better than I expected, you will find your ranking on the monitor over there, so take a short break while we prepare the pod for part two of your training." They all walked over to look at the monitor, the listing had Caalin in the number one position, Dargon second, Rostrik third, and then Clair, Jason, Faelara, Ric and Ssam. Their overall scores were extremely close so any of them could move up to any position except first, it seemed that Caalin was too far ahead of them for anyone to catch him in the next part.

Now it was time for part two of the training so everyone got back into their pods and settled into the seats. The Admiral announced, "In this part you will be flying through the rings you see in front of you as fast as you can without touching the ring with your ship. Also there will be targeting drone that you will have to shoot as you are maneuvering through the course. We will be registering how many times your ship touches one of the rings and the number of drones you hit." With that said part two began and they were all doing their best to make a perfect run."

Another two hours went by and the second part of the training was complete. Everyone was out of their pods as the Admiral entered the room, "Excellent job, you all kept it close and even changed some of your ratings but they were by a small margin." He then turned to Caalin, "And you Captain Matthews I have never had anyone get a perfect score on both part one and two I can't wait to see how you do on the finally part of your training." He then stopped for a moment, "Well I am sure you are all hungry so let's get you fed before we move on to part three."

The Admiral led them down to the dining hall and told them to enjoy their lunch he would be back later to retrieve them for the next part of their training. They found a table large enough for the eight of them and took their seats, soon one of the kitchen staff was there to take their request and within minutes had their food out for them. As they sat eating Caalin notice two crew members staring at Rostrik and Faelara and he could pretty much tell what they were talking about and it wasn't anything pleasant. It wasn't long before they got up to leave and as they walked by he heard one of them say filthy Virerians and the second one laughed and made the comment about them stinking up the ship.

Caalin quickly jumped to his feet when he felt a hand on his shoulder, "Calm down Captain Matthews remember you are the captain of your own ship and matters like these have to be dealt with diplomatically." It was Admiral Escov and he continued, "Those individuals are part of my crew so it is my responsibility to handle this so please except my apologies for their actions." Caalin calmed down, "I am sorry Admiral it was unbecoming of me." The Admiral laughed, "No worry lad when I was your age I would have knocked their blocks off myself, but don't worry you will get better as you get older and find out you can take care of problems without resorting to violence." He then turned to the lieutenant that was with him, "Get the names of those two individuals and their commanding officer and have them report to me after today's training, I think there are some special detains that need to be done and those two just volunteers for them." The lieutenant laughed, "I was wondering who we were going to get for that detail sir, I am glad they volunteered."

Caalin looked at the Admiral, "What kind of detail do you have in store for those two?" The Admiral gave Caalin a wink, "Well you see, we just dumped all the waste from our septic tank one and it needs to be scrubbed out on the inside before switch and septic tank two can be dumped, once two is dumped it will need to be scrubbed as well. I think after I am done with those two they will be a little more tolerant of other races." Caalin laughed, "I see what you mean about solving issues without violence, but isn't that a little violent in it's on right?" The Admiral broke into laughter, "Lad you are beginning to grow on me, now let's get the third and last part of your training going."

The team was led down to a shuttle bay where there were eight fighters ready to go. The Admiral pointer to a larger screen, "That is the asteroid field you will be flying through as fast as you can, but before you get worried you will have your force fields on so it will be safe." He then turned back to the team, "Now while you're flying through the field there will be targeting drones popping up all around you shooting at you, your goal is to not let them hit you before you can destroy them and not hit any of the asteroids. Your shields are set to read any hits and feed the information back to us, so load up you will be going one at a time by order of your racking from part two."

Caalin launched first making his way through the fields at a record speed taking out all the drones and not hitting a single asteroid. Next was Dargon then Rostrik, Clair, Faelara Jason, Ssam and finally Ric was the last one to take the run. After part three was over the Admiral had them all come to one of the conference rooms to go over the training results.

After everyone took their seats the Admiral spoke, "Captain Matthews you have broke our training record you are the only trainee to make it through the course with a hundred percent achievement. He then looked at the other; In fact your entire team has topped all the other people we have trained. I can say this you all passed and you have one of the best fighter squads I have ever had come through my training I am proud to know all of you."

Now that the training was over it was time for the team to head back to the Seeker, so the Admiral walked with them down to the shuttle bay to catch their shuttle back. He held his hand out and shook Caalin's, "Lad you are going to make a great admiral someday and I hope I am around when that happens." After that Caalin jumped to attention and saluted the Admiral, "Thank you sir for training and taking care of my crew while we were on board." The Admiral returned his saluted and Caalin then turned and joined his team of friends as they boarded the shuttle and lifted off heading back to the ship.

# CHAPTER 22

|||||||||||||||||||||||||||||||||||||||||||

# BACK TO THE SEEKER

Caalin and the team arrived back at the Alliance docking port and were soon transported back to the Seeker, once on board Caalin stopped on the bridge to see what had been happening while they were gone. Keyan informed him everything was quite as far as ship operations and the crew was concern, but the councilman's receptionist did contact them about a meeting tomorrow at 13:00 in his office. Caalin thanked Keyan and left to go find Ang and see if she would like to join him for dinner.

Caalin made his way to the medical facility and found Ang finishing up with an inventory so he asked her if she would like to join him for dinner. Ang did not hesitate and said yes she would, but she needed to enter her numbers into the computers before she left. Caalin waited patiently while she finished her work and then the two of them made their way to the dining hall.

Once in the dining hall the two of them ordered the daily special and Ang sat quietly while Caalin filled her in on everything about the fighter training, by the time he was done she felt like she had went through it herself. Caalin then said, "I am sorry for boring you with all my stuff, how was your day?" Ang replied, "Well after we got back from having lunch at the Lunam Amantes with Liana I came back and did an inventory of everything we had in stock in the medical facility and the last thing I did, while you were patiently waiting, was to put in an order for the things we need to replenish our stock." Caalin lowered his head," I am sorry for boring you, but thanks to your work today we will have all the medical supplies we need before we depart on our next mission."

Ang grabbed his face and looked directly into his eye, "For your information Mr. Matthews, none of the things you tell me are boring, I am happy to hear about everything you do, and yes we will be fully stocked for our next mission." Caalin laughed, "I am sorry I just thought I was boring you with the details." Ang laughed, "Ok so I take it that the entire team excelled beyond what Admiral Escov expected from you?" Caalin replied, "Yes my team set a new personal best for everyone to beat." Ang kissed him on the cheek, "I would not have expected less from you or the people that follow you." Caalin gave her a look, "What do you mean by the people that follow me?" Ang took his hand, "Have you not realized that everyone around you follows your example and in doing so they do their best, or should I say you bring out their best." Caalin scratched his head, "I don't know about that but I will admit I have a great team in the ones that volunteered."

After dinner Caalin walked Ang to her room and kissed her good night before making his way to his room to get ready for bed. The next morning he was up and having breakfast when Ssam came over to see if he had anything for him to do today. Caalin shook his head no, "I have a meeting at 13:00 with the Councilman so we may have a new mission after that but for today you are free to do what you want." After breakfast Caalin went up and spent some time on the bridge then wondered down to the shuttle bay looking over the fighters and finally stopping at the medical facility to see if Ang, Ssophia and Sisten wanted to have lunch with him before he left for his meeting.

They all went to the dining hall and got a large table and were soon joined by Dargon, Mari, Ssam, Clair, Gahe and Mouse, and they all set around talking about the fighter training. After lunch Caalin made his way off the ship and to the Councilman's office and once he entered the office the receptionist led him right on in to see the councilman. As he walked in Councilman Moreland looked up, "Caalin it is nice to see you please have a seat I have a new mission for you."

The Councilman stood up, "The information from your last mission was spot on and we were able to attack their base on Raitora, but it was not without a lost and now the pirates have declared all out war on the Alliance. They have been attacking planets and cargo ships all over. We think they also have a base on the planet Tanur and have been running raids on Proserpina so I need your crew to check it out. You can probably slip in and use one of its moons as your recon base but I need you to leave as soon as you can." Caalin stood up, "We will depart as soon as I get back to the ship and will let you know what we find." The Councilman smiled, "Thank you, I know you will do a great job and I hope you don't need those fighters I had them load on your ship for you." Caalin looked back as he was leaving, "Well sir we know how to use them if we need them."

Caalin made his way back to the Seeker and the moment he got to the bridge told Asgaya, who was on communications at the time, "Call all the officers to the briefing room and to put the rest of the crew on alert to prepare to disembark." Ten minutes later all the ship's officers were in the briefing room and Caalin walked up to the front of the room, "Everyone we have a new mission." He then went through the details of the mission then informed everyone to prepare for departure.

Within an hour the Seeker was making its way out of the docking port and through the atmosphere. Caalin then contacted Mouse and let him know they would need to go stealth before they jumped and until they land on the second moon of Tanur. Mouse let him know that there would not be a problem with that he had calibrated the stealth generator for dimensional jumps so it would not interrupt the generator at all. Caalin replied great as he turned to Ssam, "Go stealth and prepare to jump." Then he gave the commanded, "Jump." Within twenty minutes they came out of their jump still in stealth mode and made their way to Orlex the second moon of Tanor.

Once the ship had set down and was locked down Caalin decided to go have some dinner before deciding what to do next and as he was getting up he asked Ssam to join him. The two of them made their way to the dining hall and Caalin selected a two person table in the back corner away from everyone else. They took their seats and ordered their meal, and while they were waiting for the meal to come out Ssam asked Caalin why he wanted to talk to him. Caalin looked at Ssam seriously, and then whispered, "Do you remember the last time jump we made after rescuing Remus?" Ssam shook his head yes, "We took some damage and had to land on the planet Proserpina wasn't it?" Caalin looked away then back at Ssam, "Yes it was and that is where they had the memorial statues of Ang and Ssophia." He looked around once again, "That is the planet the pirates have been raiding and Tanur is where the Alliance thinks they are working out of." Ssam thought for a moment, "Ok, I get it we are going to stop it before the girls become memorial statues." Caalin pointed at Ssam, "You are one hundred percent correct the pirates stop here."

The meal came out and the two of them stopped talking until Xaera, who had brought their meal out was gone, and then Ssam ask Caalin,

"What is your plan to stop them." Caalin thought for a moment, "I don't know right now but let me sleep on it I should have a plan in mind by tomorrow." Ssam held up his tea glass as to toast Caalin, "Until tomorrow Captain."

After dinner Caalin was making his way back to his room when Ang came up behind him, "I see you have a lot on your mind, are you going to be ok?" Caalin smiled at her, "Now that I see you I think I am going to be, will you come to my room for a moment?" Ang looked a little confused but said yes and the two of them went to his room. Once they entered the room he turned, "Take a seat at the table there." Ang sat down and Caalin took a seat across the table from her, "Can I see your bracelet for a moment?" Ang still wondering what he was up to slowly took the bracelet off and handed it to him.

Caalin took the bracelet and looked at it closely, "You remember the experiment the clerk did on this thing and what he said you could do with it?" Ang shook her head, "Yes, he said if you put a magnetic field into it you could produce a force field from it." Caalin smiled, "Yes but it would have to be a strong field, stronger than anything he knew could be produced. Now gravity is basically the magnetic field of a planet and although the moon we are sitting on does not have a lot of gravity that I can manipulate I still think it will work. What if I infuse your bracelet with as much of the gravitational field that I can pull from the planet and put into it?" Ang was surprised, "If you could do that, then it should be able to produce a larger field."

Caalin held the bracelet in his hand, "Let's see if this works." He then began concentrating on the bracelet and the gravity around them and as he did so the bracelet began to glow brighter and brighter." Caalin stopped pushing gravity into the bracelet and the brightness died back down, "OK put the bracelet on and think about a force field around you." Ang put it on and began imagining a field around her and as she was doing so Caalin stood up and walked over to a chair picked up a pillow and threw it at her. Ang seeing the pillow coming at her let out a scream but the pillow hit something invisible and bounce off in the other direction."

Caalin broke into laughter, "It worked, but we don't know how big a field you can produce so come with me down to the shuttle bay where we have more room." Ang was excited about what they had discovered and followed Caalin down to the shuttle bay. When they go to the shuttle bay no one was around except for a couple of androids cleaning up. Caalin led Ang to an area where they had plenty of room, "I am going way over there and I want you to create a larger shield this time." Ang gave him a look, "You're not going to throw a wrench or something at me this time are you?" Caalin Laughed, "No I am going to have one of the droids walk toward you this time." Ang concentrated and created the field, then Caalin told one of the droids to walk over to her, but it was only able to make it a few steps in her direction until it was not able to go any closer.

Caalin then walked over to the droid and put his hand out, he could feel the force field so he followed it around Ang trying to get an idea of it size. Caalin shouted to Ang, "Ok you can stop, right now it looks like you can produce a field large enough to cover two of our large shuttles, but I think if we were outside you could produce one even larger." Caalin walked over to Ang and gave her a big kiss, "Now I will not worry about you as much as I do." Ang hugged him and whispered into his ear, "So that is why you wanted to do this, because you worry about me."

Caalin turned, "We should get back to our rooms and get some sleep we are going to have a long day tomorrow, but now I know you can protect not only yourself but people around you and that takes away some of my worries." Once they were back at Ang's room she gave him a kiss, "Good night my little worry wart and thank you for giving me something I can use not only to protect myself but my friends." She then turned and went into her room and Caalin made his way to his room to try and get a little sleep, he still had to figure out how they were going to complete their new mission.

While he was lying in his bed he received a message from Mouse, "*Caalin I just wanted you to know that before we left the Alliance base they delivered a thousand more drones to us and I have them programmed and ready to go should you want to scan the planet like we did on our last mission.*" Caalin thought for a moment, "If we use two large shuttles we can deploy the drones in both the northern and southern hemispheres and that may work for us. I will talk with Mouse first thing in the morning to get some idea on how long it will take them to complete the scan. After all that Caalin fell to sleep and got a good six hours of sleep that night.

# CHAPTER 23

||||||||||||||||||||||||||||||||||||||||||||||||||

# TANUR AND THE PIRATES

The next morning Caalin was having breakfast at 05:00 when Mouse walked in and joined him, "Did you get my message last night." Caalin nodded, "Yes and I think using the drones again is a good idea, but we will need to use two of the large shuttle to take them down, and I want to take the less number of people that I can." Mouse jumped in, "Well you will not need Ssam or Ssophia for stealth now, I have installed stealth generators on all our shuttles so we will be good there." Caalin smiled, "Great so basically we just need a pilot and an engineer, how long do you think it will take the drones to complete the survey." Mouse grinned, "Surprisingly it will only take about twelve hours, since I increased their scanning capability and their speed."

Caalin began thinking, "Ok you and Gahe will be the engineers, Dargon will take one shuttle and I will take the other." He finished his breakfast, "When I get to the bridge I will send for those two and after they eat their breakfast we will head out." Mouse stood up, "Ok I will let the kitchen staff know we will need meals for four people and meet you in the shuttle bay when you have everyone ready to go." Caalin told him ok as he left heading for the bridge while Mouse flagged down Maeria and let her know about the meals they were going to need. She nodded to Mouse, "Not a problem I will make sure they get down to the shuttles within the next twenty minutes."

Once on the bridge Caalin told Astra, "Contact Dargon, Gahe, Clair and Jason and have them meet me here on the bridge as soon as they have had their breakfast. Within thirty minutes they were all on the bridge wondering what Caalin had in mind. He asked everyone to follow him to a briefing room and then pulled up the map of Tanur, "Clair I am leaving you in charge of the bridge with Jason as your backup, Gahe you will be with me and Mouse will be with Dargon. Now here is what we are going to do; Dargon you will move to the southern hemisphere where Mouse will release his new and improved drones while Gahe and I will do the northern hemisphere. Mouse said they would only take twelve hours to complete the planet survey and we can head back if all goes well."

Dargon asked, "Why just two people per shuttle, won't we need Ssam and Ssophia for this?" Caalin shook his head, "No Mouse has installed stealth generators in all the shuttles so we will be ok without the two of them." Clair asked, "What about medical personnel, shouldn't you take them along just in case?" Caalin replied, "We are going in stealth and I don't anticipate any trouble so I do not see any need to take more people than we need, beside with the number of drones we are taking there is not enough room for more people on the shuttles, we are already taking the large shuttles as it is."

Caalin then turned to Dargon, "Now we need to find good landing stops for us to land and deploy the drones." Dargon look at the map, "Well it would need to be in an area that the pirates would never consider putting a base." Caalin thought for a moment, "You're right they would need a big enough area for all their ships and they would

CARL E. BOYETT

want to house all their personnel, so we are looking for something very narrow that not a lot of ships could get into." Jason pointed at an area on the northern hemisphere, "Here is a very narrow river valley and it looks like it goes under some over hangs in places." Clair pointed out an area in the southern hemisphere, "There is a thin valley that runs into some very narrow crevasses that you could possibly get the shuttle into."

Caalin looked over at Dargon, "I am going with the one Jason found, how do you feel about the one Clair pointed out?" Dargon looked back at the map, "Well I don't see any better options on the map so let's go with those." Caalin smile, "Great let's get down to the shuttle bay and prepare to head out." With that the five of them made their way out of the briefing room with Clair and Jason heading to the bridge and Dargon, Gahe and Caalin the shuttle bay.

When they got to the shuttle bay Mouse had already had Ekdrin and Jhevendahl load all the drones on board the shuttles. Caalin looked around, "Good job men, now Mouse your with Dargon and Gahe is with me so let's head out, go to stealth the moment we leave the ship." The shuttles fired up and they made their way off the ship as Caalin was lifting up off the moon he could see how bright the Seeker stood out on the ground, so he called back to the bridge and had Clair take the Seeker to stealth so no passing pirate ships could spot them.

Within minutes they were approaching Tanur and Caalin broke off to the north while Dargon went south and soon Caalin spotted the river and dropped down to follow it. After a few minutes he found a tight passage under an overhang that just barely had enough room to land the shuttle. Once they were on the ground the two of them pulled the drones out and deployed them. Caalin watched as they disappeared into

138

the clouds, "Well they should be back in twelve hours and we can head back so why don't we get some rest while we wait."

On the southern hemisphere Dargon found the location Clair had pointed out and eased the shuttle in very carefully scraping a few rocks as they entered. Once on the ground he and Mouse deployed their drones and they decided to set back and relax as well.

Caalin was standing at the edge of the overhang when he saw a medium pirate cruiser passing over head so he quickly made his way back to the shuttle. Gahe looked up, "What's wrong you didn't stay out there very long.: Caalin looked over at him, "Well there is definitely pirate activity on Tanur, I just saw one of their cruisers pass, and hopefully we will know their location once the drones return. Gahe looked a little scared, "Yeah maybe we should stay under the overhang just to be safe."

Twelve hours pasted and the drones started returning and both teams collected all of them and packed them away in the shuttles. Caalin fired up the shuttle and eased it out from under the overhang and went straight up leaving Tanur behind. Dargon was doing the same at his location but he seem to knock a lot of rocks loose on his way out causing Mouse to give him a hard look, "You are scratching the paint." Dargon laughed, "It is nothing a little touch up can't fix." A few minutes later as they neared the Seeker and Caalin let Clair know they were on their way in to drop the shields. Clair dropped the shield and the two shuttle came in for perfect landings in the shuttle bay then Marty called back to the bridge, "They are back on board you can bring the shields back up." With that the shield went back on line and the four shuttle member disembarked their shuttles and walked over to Marty. Caalin asked Marty, "Can you have your guy's just pull the drones off the shuttle but leave them in their containers Mouse will pull the data from them."

Caalin then turned to Mouse, "How long do you need to get the data and meet us in the briefing room?" Mouse scratched his head, "Give me fifteen minutes and I will have the data you need." Caalin replied back, "Great we will see you in the briefing room in fifteen minutes." Gahe went back to engineering while Caalin and Dargon made their way to the bridge where Caalin ask Asgaya, who was now on communications, to call all of the officers to a briefing in thirty minutes, he wanted to give Mouse a little extra time. Asgaya sent out the communications and Caalin looked over at Dargon, "Well since we have thirty minutes I want to head to the dining hall and get something cold to drink care to join me?" Then he and Dargon left and made their way down to the dining hall where they set for a few minutes discussing what the drones may have for them while enjoying a cold drink.

A few minutes later they made their way back to the bridge just as Mouse arrived to let them know he had uploaded all the data. The three of them went straight to the briefing room and Mouse brought up the data, "Well there is a large pirate base in the northern hemisphere and it is not far from where your shuttle landed." Caalin looking at the base on the hologram, "Well that will explain the cruiser that passed over our heads while we were on the planet." Mouse pointed out the movement of ships, "It looks like they are getting ready to deploy a lot of their ships and I don't know if the Alliance ships will get here in time to take them out."

Caalin studied the map for a while then turn to the other two, "Well we will have to delay them until the Alliance ships can get here." At that moment everyone else began arriving for the briefing and Caalin told Dargon and Mouse they would discuss it further during the briefing. Once everyone was seated Caalin showed them the map with the pirate base, "There is a pirate base on Tanur as the Alliance suspected, and unfortunately it looks like they are getting ready to move a lot of the ships so we need to do something to give the Alliance fleet time to get here." Clair looked at the map, "That is a big base and it's a lot of ships so what's your plan?"

Caalin thought for a moment, "I think we go in with the stealth fighters and take out and damage as many ships as we can." Mouse jumped in, "You know the minute you start firing on their ships you will have to come out of stealth as you can't fire your weapons with the shields up and that is what generates the stealth ability." Caalin looked over at Mouse and then back to the map, "With that in mind I still think that is the best course of action."

He pointed to the map, "The sun will be rising on their base in six hours so we come in from the east so they are blinded by the sun when we come out of stealth. First we take out their communications towers and the control towers and after that we have a free for all taking out the smaller ships and the engines on the cruisers." The Seeker will remain here and contact the Alliance with the data that Mouse has provided, plus you are our back up should any ships get past us."

He then looked around the room, "On the fighters it will be Ssam, Rostrik, Faelara and I." he paused, "On the Seeker Dargon will be in command, Aeron will take the port cannons, Clair will take Starboard, Jason the main gun and Resrassira on the rear cannons. Once we leave the ship with the fighters everyone will be on high alert and ready to fight." He turned to Marty, "I want your team to buckle down everything in the cargo bay that could move around we don't need things flying all over the place down there." He then turned to Jean, "I would like you and the medical team to be ready for anything, because you will need to take care of anyone that gets injured as quickly as possible."

Before he called the meeting to an end he turned to Mouse one last time, "I want you to check and double check the fighters they are the key to pulling everything off." Mouse looked Caalin straight in the eyes, "Don't worry I will make sure everything is ready." Caalin then told everyone, "Ok it is a go in six hours so get some rest if you can we may be in for a long hard fight."

As everyone was leaving he called his fighter team over and the four of them set down and studied the map and the data that Mouse had added. Caalin looked at a valley that ran east to west just a little south of where he would like to attack from and he pointed it out, "If we come through this valley fling as low as we can we should be able to pop up over this ridge and surprise them." Ssam looked at the map, "That seems like a good plan but the minute we start firing on them they are going to be able to see us." Caalin set back in his chair, "You remember the asteroid field exercise during our training, well we will have to fly a lot faster than that this time and I don't want any of you losing one of my fighters." He then stood up, "Ok everyone go get something to eat and get some rest we don't know how long this battle will take and I want you rested up for it."

# CHAPTER 24

||||||||||||||||||||||||||||||||||||||||||||

# DRAGON BATTLE
# (BANGALOR DARGON
# VS. RED DRAGON)

It was 04:00 when Caalin walked into the dining hall and saw Dargon, Clair, Jason and his fighter team all having breakfast together before the mission. He made his way over and Join them, "It is nice to see you all getting a good meal before the action starts." Dargon looked over at Caalin, "I think once your team launches we need to pull the Seeker up off Orlex but keep the moon between us and Tanur while we stay in stealth mode." Caalin thought for a moment, "That is a good idea, then you will be able to move at a moment's notice should any other cruisers arrive, but I want you to know if it looks like you have no chance in a fight you are to jump out of the arena and get to Alliance space, I don't want to lose my ship and crew to a bad decision." Dargon relucticly agree to Caalin's demands and they all continue eating there meal.

After breakfast Caalin's team started making their way down to the shuttle bay and there ships. Before Ssam could get out of the dining hall door Clair grabbed him, gave him a kiss and hugged him tight whispering into his ear, "You had better comeback in one piece or I will never forgive you." Ssam squeezed her closer, "I will do my best so you do yours and keep the ship safe." Clair wiped a tear from her eyes, "You know I will silly." After that Ssam left to catch up with the others. Before Caalin went to the shuttle bay he made a stop by the medical facility to see Ang. She met him at the entrance and threw her arms around him telling him, "Now Mr. Matthews I don't want you playing the hero out there I just want you to come back safe." Caalin smiled, "I will see you sooner than you think we got this." He then gave her a kiss and ran off to the shuttle bay.

In the shuttle bay he gave his team one last briefing, "We will have to fly in single file as we fly through the valley so once we leave the ship turn your beacons on to keep track of each other's position I don't want us running in to one another out there. I will lead everyone through the valley so stay close and once we come out of the valley we go live and will no longer have our stealth. So the last things you need to know is hit them hard, hit them fast, and get back alive, I will not have anyone getting killed on my watch." The entire team jumped to attention and in unison shouted, "YES SIR!" Caalin then shouted, "Load up team and let's go!"

Once everyone were in their fighters they fired up the engines and went through their systems check after a couple of minutes Caalin came over the communications system, F1 ready to launch. A few seconds later Ssam replied F2 ready, then Rostrik F3 ready and finally Faelara F4 ready. Caalin came back, "Let's launch and go to stealth once we are out of the bay."

All the fighters pulled out of the shuttle bay turning on their locator beacons and going stealth the moment they were clear the ship. Caalin led them as they headed down toward the planet, then once inside the atmosphere they got as low as they could and flew as close to the ground as possible. Within minutes they came to the opening to the valley and dove down into it flying at extremely high speeds. Ssam was sweating as he could see how close the valley walls were and one slight mistake in one of the turns and he would be eating one of those walls.

Finally Caalin pulled up out of the valley right into the pirate base with the other three fighters right behind him. Caalin called to the others, I am going for the control tower, Ssam take out their communications, Rostrik and Faelara start taking out the ships on the ground, and don't let any of them get off the ground." Rostrik and Faelara began blasting the ships on the ground as Caalin and Ssam did their part with both the control and communication towers, and then began firing on the ships on the ground. Only a few small ships got off the ground but were intercepted by the Seeker once they left the atmosphere.

While Caalin and his team were wrapping up the fighting on Tanur, Dargon transmitted, "F1 the Seeker has received a call for assistance from Proserpina they are being attacked by a medium pirate cruise and it fighters. The Seeker is in route to help so you need to catch up as soon as you can." Ssam recognized the planet's name, "Caalin did he say Proserpina?" Caalin came back with, "Yes so we need to finish here as fast as we can." After hearing the message Caalin was more determined to wrap his mission up and was hitting everything he could on the ground then with thirty minutes of dodging ground fire they had disabled or destroyed every ship on the ground leaving the pirate crewmember stranded on the ground for the Alliance Ground Forces to deal with once they arrive.

Caalin gave the command to his team, "Ok we head to Proserpina to help the Seeker deal with the pirates there." They pointed their fighter to the sky and upward they went leaving the atmosphere and speeding toward their next battle. As they got closer they could see the Seeker in a battle with the medium cruiser and it looked like they were winning. Caalin called Dargon, "How are you guys holding out." Dargon replied, "We are ok, could use a little help, we sent a medical team down to the planet to assist with the injured, but there's still some fighters down there making it hard for them." Caalin came back, "Who was on the medical team went down?" Dargon came back with, "It was Ang and Ssophia, and Ric flew them down in one of the small shuttles."

Caalin was shocked as he thought to himself that this was his worst nightmare coming back to haunt him. He then barked out orders over the communications system, "Ssam and Faelara assist the Seeker, Rostrik you are with me we have some pirate fighters to take out down on the planet." After that Caalin turned his fighter toward the planet and flew as fast as he could get it to go making it hard for Rostrik to keep up with him. Caalin remembered from the time jump what village was being attacked and flew straight for it then as he got closer he spotted three fighters and took them on in combat. Within a minute he had destroyed two of the fighters and was going after the last one when he notices Ang and Ssophia on the ground helping several injured people. The Pirate fighter dove straight at them firing it guns and blast were going off all over the area they were in. Caalin screamed, "NO!" Then he blasted the pirate fighter out of the sky.

Caalin turned his fighter around and made his way back to the location he saw Ang and the others. Tears ran down his face as he saw Ang using the bracelet to produce a force field that protected not only herself and Ssophia but everyone she was trying to save. Caalin quickly brought his fighter down next to them and jumped out running to meet Ang. He had tears running down his face when he finally reached her and she smiled at him as she wiped his face, "It is ok, there will be no memorial statues going up, Ssophia and I are ok thanks to you and your magical bracelet."

Caalin kissed Ang then whispered, "I thought my worst nightmare had come true and I had lost you forever." Ang held him tight, "Well you don't have to worry about that nightmare any longer." Rostrik landed nearby and came over, "Well that was a waste, you tell me to follow you and then you take them all out by yourself. I just got a communications from Dargon, they defeated the pirate cruiser and the Alliance force just arrived in the area, he would like to know what you want him to report to them." Caalin replied, "Tell him we are on our way back to the ship and to have one of the large shuttles loaded with medical supplies, we will need to bring Jean and Sisten back down here to help with the injured." Rostrik returned to his fighter communicating the message back to the Seeker as Caalin turned to Ang, "I will be back with more supplies and help so do your best until then." Ang smiled at him, "I will be waiting for you so don't take too long." Caalin made it back to his fighter and lifted off heading back to the Seeker.

Once back on board he contacted the command ship of the Alliance fleet informing them of the pirate that were still on the ground on Tanur and that his people were going to stay where they were for now to provide medical assistance to the people on Proserpina. The fleet commander told Caalin that was a good idea and that the Alliance Council had requested they return to port once they have wrapped things up here. Caalin confirmed that once they have provided the adequate medical assistance that they would return to headquarters.

Caalin flew the shuttle down to the planet with Jean and Sisten and all the medical supplies they could get on the ship. Marty flew down with all his crew plus all the androids that Mouse had reprogrammed to help with search and rescue of people trapped under rubble. Later Tehaena came down with Orianna, Xaera and Jhalia from the kitchen with food for all the hard workers. Jhalia whispered to Caalin, "Belrion wanted to be the one coming down but Tehaena would not let him." Caalin laughed, "Well we know who wears the pants in that relationship don't we." Jhalia broke into laughter, "I guess you're right about that."

Two days later and everything was wrapping up and the Seeker crewmembers were being flown back up to the ship. Caalin was taking with the Mayor of the village who was thanking him for all their help saving not only the village but the people that live there. The Mayor looked over at Ang and Ssophia as they were telling everyone goodbye, "Those two girls risked their lives out there helping the injured and protecting them, do you think it would be ok if we put up statues honoring the two of them?" Caalin smiled at the Mayor, "Sir it would be more than ok, and if you need any help be it for materials or financing please contact me, those two deserve to be honored."

Caalin wave to the Mayor as he entered the shuttle and then made his way to the pilot seat. Ang came over and set next to him in the copilot seat and asked, "What were you and the Mayor talking about you seemed to be happy about whatever it was." Caalin reached over and patted her hand, "Let's just say those statues that were in my nightmares will not be memorial statues anymore but they will still be there to honor the two of you." The shuttle then lifted off the ground and they headed back to the ship.

# CHAPTER 25

||||||||||||||||||||||||||||||||||||||||||||||

# THE RESCUE

Once back on board the Seeker Caalin made his way back to the bridge and once he was seated Keyan turned to him, "We have a communications from the Alliance Fleet Commander he stated that they have received a distress signal from the Deilon system but his troops are still wrapping up with the pirate on the ground at Tanur so he is asking us to check it out before heading back to headquarters." Caalin replied, "Do we have the location for the signal?" Keyan nodded, "Yes he sent them along." He turned to Evalon who was on navigation, "Plug in the location and prepare to jump." Within second they had made the jump and were soon in the Deilon system.

Caalin asked Clair, "Scan the area for a ship in distress there is no telling where it may have drifted." Clair quickly came back with, "We have a vessel four hundred kilometers off our port bow." Caalin looked over at Keyan again, "Let's make our way to that ship." Minutes later they had the ship in sight and Caalin could see it was an old pirate slave ship that was just drifting in space. Caalin stood up, "Clair you have the helm, Dargon you and Jason are with me." The three of them made their way down to the shuttle bay and took one of the large shuttles and made their way over to the old ship. Caalin brought the shuttle up next to the ship and lock on to one of the external hatches then secured the seal around it then forced the hatch on the ship open.

The ship was dark and dirty with lights flickering all around, Caalin told Jason and Dargon to be on their toes this was a pirate ship. The three of them made their way to the bridge and found a half starve woman leaning over the communications system. She slowly lifted her head and saw the three of them, "Thank goodness my signal got out." Caalin looked at her, "What happened here?" All the woman could say was, "The others are below." After getting those words out of her mouth she passed out. Caalin pulled his communicator out and called back to the Seeker, "We need a medical team over here as soon as possible also have Mouse and Gahe accompany them, tell them connect to our shuttle and come inside through that port." Keyan replied, "I will contact engineering and medical now."

Caalin turned to Jason, "Can you get her back to our shuttle while Dargon and I check below?" Jason nodded, "I will take care of her and once the medical team gets here I will come find you." Jason picked the woman up and carried her in the direction of their shuttle while Caalin and Dargon found a stairway that lead down to the lower level. Once on the lower level the smell was almost suffocating and they were horrified by what they found, there were cages down both sides of the ship, two of the cages had dead bodies in them and there were five people that were barely alive in the others.

Caalin was not able to open the cage doors because none of the power to them worked. He looked over at Dargon, "We will need Mouse down here to open these doors." Dargon agreed to go back and bring Mouse down when he got there and Caalin told him, "Bring anyone else that can help carry these people out of here." One of the people was able to talk so Caalin asked what happen. She looked up at him, "Arria did it, she got out and was able to call for help thank goodness we are saved." Again Caalin asked, "Can you tell me what happed here?" She paused for a moment, "The pirates they abandon us, they heard something about the Alliance taking out one of their bases and they took the shuttle and fled. We have not had food or water for three days, I think, it is hard to keep track of time here."

Caalin then told her, "Save your energy we will get you out of here and over to our ship so just be patient." The moment Caalin had finish that sentence Dargon was back with Mouse, Jason, and Gahe. Caalin turn to Mouse can you do something about these locks. Mouse turned and grabbed the door with his bionic arm and snatched it open then looked at Caalin, "That takes care of that one I will get the others." As he opened the doors one of the others would take the person and carry them up to the waiting shuttles where Ang and Jean were to check their medical condition. After they had all the abandon slaves and the bodies of the dead on board the shuttles they made their way back to the Seeker.

Back on ship they took all six women to the medical facility to be taken care of as Caalin was about to leave he told Jean to let him know the minute they are able to eat something and he would have them bring some food down from the kitchen. Jean nodded, "That would be great I don't think I want to move them right away, but in the mean time can you have them prepare some rooms for them once they are better." Caalin smiled, "I will take care of that and let you know when the rooms are ready."

On the way back to the bridge Caalin stopped by the kitchen to inform Belrion and Tehaena about the new passengers, he explained that once they were well enough to eat that he would like for them to take some food down to the medical facility for them. Tehaena told him that they would take care of it and make sure that the women were fed well. Caalin thanked them and went on to the bridge were he asked Clair if she could have rooms prepared for their new guest because once they were able he wanted to move them from medical to their own rooms. Clair assured him that she would take care of it immediately then headed out to do so. Clair informed him That Marty's team had moved the bodies of the two that had passed to a storage area and covered them with sheets. Caalin thanked her for the information.

Caalin took his seat and stared out at the old pirate ship that had housed those women that were to be sold as slaves and the more he looked at it the angrier he got. He then turned to Dargon, "Lock all forward guns on that ship and fire until it is gone from my sight." Dargon turn the cannons and locked them onto the pirate ship and began firing and in less than a minute is was nothing but a debris field. Caalin still angry, "Now that's a better sight." He then got up from his seat, "Dargon you have the helm I need to cool off a bit." Caalin walked off the bridge and Keyan turned to Dargon, "I have never seen Caalin get that angry before." Dargon just lowered his head, "You did not see what we saw on that ship, I wanted to do the same thing but I am glad he did, it will give him a little relief from his pain."

Caalin made his way to the dining hall and took a seat in the darkness corner he could find; once he was seated Maeria came over and asked what he would like. Caalin just asked her to bring him a cup of tea he just wanted to set awhile in a nice quite place and think. She brought his tea out and he just set there staring at it for about thirty minutes without taking a single sip from the cup. Soon Maeria came back over and informed him, "We are sending food down to medical for the new guest since they are well enough to eat now and Jean stated that one of them wishes to talk to you."

Caalin stood up and thanked her for the tea then made his way down to the medical facility where all the girls were eating. The sight of them enjoying a meal put a smile on his face for the first time since he came back on board after their rescue. Jean met him as he walked in, "Arria is the one that requested to speak with you so be gentle she still doesn't have all her strength back yet." Caalin looked at her, "Jean I will let her tell me about what happened to them at her on pace, I promise not to push her for the information." Jean smiled, "I know you will."

Caalin walked over and took a seat next to the girl called Arria, "Well it is good to see you eating and getting stronger, I understand your name is Arria correct?" She looked at Caalin with worried eyes, "Yes it is Arria, Arria Phelar." Caalin smiled, "Ok Arria can you tell me about you girls and why you were abandon on that ship?" Arria started crying, "That ship, that horrible ship I wish I could destroy it." Caalin reached over and turned on a monitor screen and switch it to an outside view so she could see the debris floating around, "I'm sorry if I had known sooner I would have let you give the command to destroy it, but I got a little angry and did it myself." Arria stared at the monitor then began to laugh, "You know you are a funny man, I think I like you." Caalin lowered his voice, "Not so loud that is my girlfriend is over there and she is get very jealous when people talk to me like that." Arria's laughter got louder and Ang came over, "Caalin what are you telling this young lady, you know she is trying to get her strength back and you don't need to excite her that much." Arria looked at Ang, "He told me that you were his girlfriend and was the jealous type." Ang smack Caalin on the arm, "Why would you tell her that? Caalin smiled, "I am not going to lie to her, and you can't tell me with a straight face that you have never gotten jealous."

Ang turned to Arria, "Well yes I am his girlfriend and yes I have gotten a little jealous at times, but he was the cause of it all." Arria smile, "I can see that, he is handsome and witty, but he is taken so you have no worries about me." She then looked at Caalin, "From what I can make out you are in charge of this ship?" Caalin nodded, "Yes I am Captain Caalin Matthews the commander of this ship AS1-Seeker and we are part of the Alliance Fleet." She smiled, "Then I think I can trust you." She continued, "All of us are from the planet Kileshan and were captured in a raid on our village. We were the only one left alive, the entire village was massacred and we were taken to be sold off as slaves."

She began pointing around the room at the girls telling Caalin their names, "She is Phyla Ruther, and that is Mylae Ludra, that girl is Aethia Toryn and she is Elice Bhader and the last one over there is Takaria Phelk." She lowered her head, "The two that did not make it were Huira Tohyl and Estala Irsap they pass away a couple of days ago from injuries inflected by those awful pirates." She continued, "From what I could hear the pirates were talking about a war and that they were not going to get caught on a slave ship so they took the only shuttle they had and abandon us still lock in our cages." She took a drink of water, "After a lot of trying, I finally got my cage door to open and made my way up to the bridge, but I did not know how to operate the communication system but I was finally able to find the distress signal and activate it and you came to rescue us, thank you."

Caalin stood up, "Well that is enough talking for you for now, we have rooms ready for all of you and Ang will make sure you are all escorted to your own room." He then turned to Ang, "I have to get back on the bridge we will be making a jump back to Alliance Headquarters soon so take care of our guest please." Ang smiled at him, 'You can count on me I will make sure they all get settled in." Caalin turned to leave, "Arria get better we can talk again later." After he was gone Arria turned to Ang, "You have a nice boyfriend so you better hang on to him, he's a keeper." Ang nodded, "That he is."

Once Caalin was back on the bridge he took his seat, "Contact Alliance Headquarters and let them know we are headed home and that I need to meet with Councilman Moreland once we are back." He then looked over at Ric on navigations, "Prepare to jump." Ric replied, "Ready for jump on your command." Caalin pointed into space, "Jump." Within thirty minutes they came out of there jump in Alliance space seven hundred kilometers from base.

Keyan turned to Caalin, "They have given us the go ahead to approach, we will be using the same docking port as before and the Councilman will meet with you the moment we get docked and secured." Caalin smiled, "Ok take us in I have a meeting to attend." They made their way down to the planet and into the docking port and once the ground crew had everything locked down Caalin departed for his meeting.

# CHAPTER 26

|||||||||||||||||||||||||||||||||||||||||||||||||||

# BACK AT HQ

Caalin made it to Councilman Moreland's office where the receptionist took him right on in and Moreland stood up, "Have a seat lad I have been hearing good things about your ship and crew." Caalin took his seat and the Councilman continued, "I understand that you took your fighters in and grounded all the pirate ships on their base minus the few that the Seeker took out, then you took out the pirates that attacked Proserpina and rendered medical assistance to the village. I got a lot of messages from the leaders of that planet; I understand they are putting up statues of Angiliana and Ssophia for their bravery. Now the only thing I don't have any information on is the distress call you answered before returning, would you care to fill me in on that?"

Caalin went into detail about the pirate slave ship and the girls they rescued, but unfortunately two of them had passed away before they got to them. He then ask the Councilman, "Would you take the bodies of those two and make sure they are given a proper burial and if possible on their home planet with the rest of their village." The Councilman nodded his head, "You did not need to ask we will be happy to take care of their remains and see to it they get their proper honors."

Caalin then asked, "What will be done with the six I still have on board the Seeker?" The Councilman scratched his head, "Well it will take a few days to arrange housing for them here so if you do not mind can they stay on you ship while the arrangements are being made." Caalin replied, "No that is perfectly fine with me and my crew, it will give us time to get to know them better, but then what will happen to them?" The Councilman thought for a moment, "Well it will depend on them whether or not they want to go back to their home planet or stay here. If they choose to stay here and don't have any skills to provide for themselves we will set them up with training to help them." He then stood up, "Give your crew some needed time off they deserve it after that mission, I should have a new mission and have the house setup for the six girls in a few days, I will let you know."

Caalin made his way back to the ship and once on board went to let Ang know what he had discussed with the councilman, as he entered the medical facility he noticed all the girls were gone. He looked around and found Ang, "I see you must have gotten our guest moved to their rooms." Ang nodded, "Yes and since we got their measurements, while we were examining them, we were able to get them some fresh clothes to wear other than those old rags they had on. All the girls on board donated clothing for them and you should have seen the smiles on their faces." Caalin smiled at Ang, "I am proud of you and the others that was a wonderful thing you did for them."

He then cleared his throat, "Well it seems like they will be with us for a little longer until the councilman can arrange housing for them so we will need someone to show them around and introduce them to the rest of the crew." There was a voice from behind the two of them, "I would be happy to show them around." It was Marjori Kai and she continued, "I haven't had a lot to do lately and Ang has her medical

157

duties to do around here so I would be happy to escort our new guest." Caalin smiled at Marjori, "I would greatly appreciate it if you did, I want to make them feel at home here and I know you can do that." Marjori winked at Caalin, "You can count on me to make sure of it, so I will go check on them now."

Caalin turned to Ang, "Would you like to join me in the dining hall for a cup of tea and maybe a desert if they have some available?" Ang looked around, "Give me a few minutes I have some things to finish up here and I will join you afterwards if that is ok?" Caalin winked at her, "Then I will see you in a little while so go finish your work." Caalin turned and head to the bridge to inform Dargon, Clair, and Jason about what he and the councilman had discussed for their six guests."

After he had informed the three of them about everything he and Councilman Moreland has discussed Clair made a suggestion, "Why don't we ask the ladies if they would like to train with some of our personnel to get a head start on finding out what they would like to do, I know Keyan would be happy to train them on communications and maybe they could learn navigations or help as Med Tech with Ang's team." Caalin thought for a moment, "I think that would be a great idea, why don't you get with Marjori and the two of you talk to the ladies to see if that is something they would like to do, I don't want them to feel obligated to do it. Marjori has taken the task of showing them around the ship and introducing them to the crew so she can be your liaison with the girls."

Clair was excited, "Great I will get with Marjori right away so we can talk to the girls, and we will not pressure them into anything." Caalin laughed, "Great, and I know you will not pressure them, now I am heading to the dining hall to meet Ang for some tea so if you need me for anything that is where you can find me." Clair jumped back in, "Tell Ang to try Tehaena's prezeanip pudding it is fantastic." Caalin waved as he left the bridge, "I will tell her you suggested it."

Caalin made it to the dining hall and had ordered the tea and the pudding that Clair suggested and was setting at a corner table when Ang arrived. Ang made her way over and took a seat apologizing for make him wait so long. Caalin put his hand on hers, "I just got here myself, so no need for apologies; I have ordered the tea and a desert that Clair stated you had to try." She perked up, "Well if Clair says I need to try it then it must be good."

Maeria brought the tea and desert out, "Tehaena said she hopes you enjoy the prezeanip pudding she has only been able to get the ingredients for it since we got back." Ang took a quick taste of it, "This is awesome, tell her I hope she will keep being able to get the ingredients for it." Caalin took a bite of his, "She is right this is wonderful, give Tehaena my compliments for a wonderful desert." Maeria smiled, "I will, she will be twilled with it coming from the two of you." She turned and headed to the kitchen to let Tehaena know as Ang and Caalin enjoy their desert and tea.

Caalin looked up and saw Marjori and they six girls walk into the dining hall, he had not seen the girls since they had time to clean up and get dressed in new clothes so he was shocked to see how pretty they all were and he thought to himself, *"Their looks must be the reason the pirate took them to sell as slaves."* Although they all were from the same village they were all completely different in their looks. Three of the girls, Arria, Mylae, and Takaria were all small petite girls; Arria had a tan skin tone with blonde hair and bright pale green eyes that seem to sparkle when she looked at you. Mylae had very pale skin, jet black hair and brown eyes while Takaria had very light green skin, bright green eyed and dark green hair and could have been a relative of Ssophia and Ssam.

Then there was the other three, Phyla was the tallest of them all with her dark skin, bright silvery blue eyes and brown hair. The two others were medium height, Aethia had a reddish tone to her skin, black hair and dark purple eyes, but Elice had pale blue skin, dark eyes and hair. They were all beautiful in their own way and Caalin could not help noticing it. Marjori brought the ladies over to introduce them to Caalin since the only one he really had time to talk to was Arria.

Marjori turned to the girls, "Ladies this is Captain Caalin Matthews the commander of this ship and the one who led the team that rescued all of you, he is the youngest ship commander in Alliance history and was one of my favorite students when we were at Boldoron Academy." Arria spoke up, "I have already had the honor of talking with Captain Matthews and I find him to be extremely pleasant and easy to talk to, plus he is very handsome, but he is taken so get any ideas of flirting with him out of your minds." Ang laughed and gave Arria thumbs up for her comment. Caalin just shook his head, "Ladies you all can just call me Caalin as long as you are on this ship you will be treated like family that is how we all treat each other here."

All the girls made it a point to thank Caalin for their rescue and telling him how nice his crew has been treating them since they have been on board, but they did not know how they could repay him for all they have done for them. Caalin looked at them all, "Ladies you owe us nothing for doing something that any descent person would have done and I want you to know we are trying to bring the pirates to justice for all their crimes." He then asked Marjori if Clair had talked with her and

Marjori insured him she had and her and the ladies were on their way to the briefing room next to set down with Clair and talk.

Caalin smiled, "Great I can't wait to hear how things go, so I will talk to Clair later." He then turned back to the girls, "You ladies enjoy the rest of your tour and when you make it to dinner later try some of Tehaena's prezeanip pudding it is fantastic." Ang jump in, "I can vouch for that the pudding is great." The girls turned to leave and Arria waved back to Ang, "I will see you later Angiliana." Ang smile and waved back, "Later Arria." Caalin looked over at Ang, "I see you have made another good friend." Ang smiled, "Yeah she is a nice girl and is slowly coming out a little more after all they went through." Caalin replied, "I just wished we could have caught the pirates that abandon them to die and brought them to justice." Ang placed her hand on Caalin's arm, "You can't let that get to you the important thing here is that they are all safe now."

# CHAPTER 27

||||||||||||||||||||||||||||||||||||||||||

# THE DECISIONS OF
# THE SIX GUEST

Marjori escorted the girls to the briefing room to meet with Clair, and as they entered they were ask to take a seat. Once everyone was seated Clair began, "Ladies I have talked with Caalin about your situation and it seems it may be days before the Alliance council can arrange housing for you on the base, so they have asked us to allow you to stay on board until they have the housing ready. Caalin made it clear that you ladies are welcome to stay on board as long as you wish and has asked me to assist you with anything you need. I have suggested to him that we help you get some type of training that could help you get jobs to allow you to support yourselves once you leave us, so if there is any positions on board you would like to learn about please speak up and I will coordinate the training for you."

Takaria spoke up, "I think I would love to learn how to operate the communication system, if that is not a problem?" Elice jumped in, "I am interested in that as well if it is ok for both of us to do it?" Clair smiled at her, "It doesn't matter how many of you want to learn a particular job we will train you all in whatever you like." Mylae looked over at Aethia and the two of them together said, "We would like to learn navigations." Clair nodded to them, "Then navigations it is."

Arria and Phyla sat talking for a moment then Arria spoke for both of them, "We would like to train with the security team, we both want to get stronger and be able to protect ourselves and others." Marjori jumped in before Clair could say anything, "I think that would be wonderful, but I would like to train all of you in self defense on top of your other training." Clair agreed with Marjori, "You two can learn from my team and all of you can train with Marjori for self defense and don't worry she taught it back at Boldoron Academy and was my instructor there so I vouch for her training."

Clair stood up, "Well if Mylae, Aethia, Elice and Takaria if you will come with me I will introduce you to the officers in charge of communications and navigations." She looked over to the other two girls, "If you will go with Marjori she will introduce you to the rest of the security team and you can began getting a feel of what they do on board." Marjori then said, "Once we have everyone's training schedules I will set up class time for the self defense training."

Clair took her group to the bridge and introduced Mylae and Aethia to Ssam and then introduced Elice and Takaria to Keyan. The girls were happy to talk with them and both Keyan and Ssam immediately began showing each group things that they would be trained on.

Caalin appeared on the bridge and the moment he took his seat Ssam turned to him, "You know we can get these ladies trained on the basic operations of these systems, but without some actual experience in space they will only be familiar with the equipment." Caalin thought for a moment, "I think I need a meeting with Councilman Moreland and see if there are any escort missions or transport mission we can do to give them the training they will need." He then turns to Keyan, "Would you please contact the councilman's office and set up a meeting for me?" Keyan smiled, "I would be happy to; it will give me a chance to show these ladies how to do that."

Before Keyan could contact the councilman's office Marty called up from the shuttle bay and asked if Caalin would come down they have a new delivery he needed to see. Caalin replied, "I am on my way down, Keyan let me know when you have the meeting scheduled." He then left the bridge and made his way down to the shuttle bay. Once there Marty pointed at the young ground crewman standing on the ramp, "That young man has some papers for you to sign."

Caalin walked over and asked the young man, "I hear you need my signature for something?" The crewman jumped to attention, "Yes sir, we are delivering four new fighters for you to go with the others you have. The Alliance Council decided since you have eight trained fighter pilots you should have ships for all of them." Caalin rubbed his head, "OK, but we will need a little more time to make room for them, do they have to be delivered today?" The Crewman replied, "No sir just let us know when you have made room for them and we can bring them over to you." Caalin signed for the fighter and told the crewman, "We will contact you when we have the shuttle bay ready for their arrival."

The crewman turned and left and Caalin turned to Marty, "Do you think we can make room in here for four more fighters?" Marty looked around, "If you can get us a lift to use we can stack some of this cargo containers in the cargo bay clearing up a lot of room, it is such a mess in here because we have never had a proper lift to move things with." Caalin put his hand on Marty's shoulder, "Well I am scheduling a meeting with Councilman Moreland so I will put a lift on the top of my list to talk to him about." Marty smiled, "OK while you are trying to get us a lift we will move what we can around and see if there is any way to make the room you need." Caalin thanked him and then headed back toward the bridge to see if Keyan had been able to set up the meeting.

On his way back he walked past the armory where Faelara was talking to Arria and Phyla about the weapons they had on board. Faelara spotted Caalin and called to him, "Caalin may I have a word with you?" Caalin stopped, "Yes what can I do for you?" Faelara pointed to the weapons, "We do not have a facility for weapons training and I think that not only the security team but all the crew members should be trained on how to use each of the weapons we have, and to be somewhat proficient with them." Caalin thought for a moment, "We don't have room for any type of weapons training on board; well I have a meeting coming up with the councilman so I will bring it up with him, it will be the third item on my list." Faelara smiled, "That would be great thank you."

Caalin finally made it back to the bridge where Keyan informed him that the councilman would see him today as soon as he could get over to his office. Caalin replied, "Contact them and let them know I am on my way now." He made his was off the ship and down to the dock where he flagged a crewman to drive him over to the councilman's office. Once he was at the office the receptionist looked up, "Go on in Captain Matthews the councilman is waiting for you."

Caalin entered the room and was greeted by Councilman Moreland, "Caalin my lad what do I owe this honor too?" Caalin took his seat, "Sir I have a few request I need to run by you." Moreland smiled, "Well let's hear those request and I will see what we can do to help you out." Caalin set back, "Well first I would like to request a lift for our cargo bay, we are unable to stack cargo and the bay is getting crowded, we don't have enough room for the four new fighters we are receiving." The Councilman looked surprised, "I was not aware you did not have a lift, but I will have two sent over immediately, what's next on your list?

Caalin cleared his throat, "Well since Arria and the other girls are remaining on our ship until proper housing has been arranged we decided to give them some training that could benefit them in getting positions to support their selves once they have the housing. We let the girls decide what they wanted training on and two of them selected navigations, two of them selected communications and the other two wanted to work in security, so we have assigned each of them to the appropriate teams to train. The problem is we cannot give them any practical training setting in port we need some type of small mission, be it transport or escort, to take them out for better training."

The Councilman laughed, "That was a great idea, but I will need to look at what missions we have and get back to you on that are there anything else I can help you with?" Caalin replied, "Yes I have one more, The security team has asked if there was any place to train personnel on the use of all the weapons we have on board, they have suggested that everyone on board get training on the proper use of the weapons." The Councilman smiled, "I think your security team is right about that, let me do some checking and get back to you, I should have some answers by tomorrow, but I will have your lifts over to you today." Caalin thanked the councilman for his time and made his way out of the office and back to the Seeker.

As Caalin was walking along the walkway heading for the ramp Marty shouted to him, "Hey Caalin great job they just delivered two lifts to us and I only asked for one." Caalin shouted back, "Great now get those cargo containers stored properly and let me know when we have room for them to deliver the fighters." He made his way back on board and to the bridge where he informed Keyan that the councilman was checking on missions they could do and will let them know something tomorrow. After that he made his way down to the cargo bay stopping by the armory to catch Faelara up on the meeting with the councilman. Then finally to the cargo bay to see how much room they were getting by stacking the cargo containers.

After a while Marty's team had the shuttle bay clear of all cargo and they had plenty of room for both the shuttles and the fighters including the new ones they were getting. They moved all the shuttles to the port side and lined them along the wall, then move the fighters to the starboard side and did the same; this left plenty of room for the four new fighters on the starboard side with plenty of room down the middle to move cargo. It would also allow the fighter and shuttles to move through when taking off and landing with no issues.

Caalin was admiring their work when Marty walked up beside him, "Looks great doesn't it?" Caalin smiled, "It looks fantastic, now I can let them know they can deliver the new fighters tomorrow, if that is ok with you?" Marty laughed, "We have more than enough room now so why do you need my approval?" Caalin turned to leave slapping Marty on the shoulder, "I just wanted to make sure my Cargo Officer was good with it."

It was now late and Caalin was getting hungry so he decided he would head to dinner, but on the way he stopped on the bridge and sent a message over to have the fighters delivered the next day. As he walked into the dining hall he spotted Ang, Ssophia and Sisten with Arria and the other girls setting at a table so he decided not to bother them and went over and set down with Mouse, Dargon and Ssam. Nasth came over and took Caalin's order and went to get his food. Caalin looked over at Mouse, "We have four new fighters arriving tomorrow, would you mind giving them a look over and see what you might need to do to improve them." Mouse smile, "I would love too, I love improving Alliance equipment."

He then looked over to Dargon, "I have asked for some missions that would allow us to train the new girls better and we are just waiting on the councilman to get back with me on it. I also requested a training area for weapons training for everyone; we all need to be able to operate the weapons we have on board." Dargon nodded, "I think you are right about that, with the rise of conflicts with the pirates we need to me prepared for the worst."

Mouse thought for a moment, "Yeah once I have learned how the weapons work I may even be able to improve them as well." Caalin laughed, "Why don't you just stick to the fighters for now we will discuss the others at a later date." Mouse replied, "OK, at least you didn't shoot the idea down completely." Caalin came back with, "No I didn't and with the pirates attacking every ship they can I am not going to stop you from making improvements to any of our weapons."

# CHAPTER 28

# TRAINING MISSION

The next morning after a nice breakfast with Ang, Caalin made his way down to the shuttle bay and the new fighters had just arrived and were being loaded on board. He walked around looking them over, they were that same as the four they already had, so he knew Mouse would have no issues installing the stealth generators on them. As he was watching Councilman Moreland walked up, "I see you are checking out the new fighters, I'm sorry but they are the same as the ones you already have, I wanted to give you some of the newer ones but the council voted it down, something about it would not be fair giving you all the new equipment since you have not been a commander of a ship as long as some of the older commanders." Caalin laughed, "It doesn't bother me, we will make do with whatever you can give us, you forget I have a great engineer team." The councilman laughed, "That you do."

Caalin then asked, "What brings you by this morning I know it wasn't to watch them load the fighters." Moreland looked over at Caalin, "You are so right, I have the training mission and weapons training you asked for, it is all in one mission." He walked over and gave Caalin a disc, "All the information is on this disc, but I will tell you the bulk of it. We have a weapons training base on Spiria, you will travel there at warp speed and no jumps so it will take you about three days to get there which should give the girls plenty of training. The disc holds a few route changes along the way for the navigation training and once you are at Spiria Admiral Madison will be the man to meet for the weapons training, he is aware that you are coming so they will be ready for you."

The Councilman turned to walk off, "Oh I forgot to tell you that you are to depart first thing in the morning and be careful out there we have received reports of pirate cruisers jumping in and out of Alliance space attacking any vessel they run across." Caalin replied, "Thank you for your help we will be gone in the morning before you are up and about, and we will stay on alert." Caalin took the disc and made his way toward the bridge to share the information.

Once on the bridge he asked Elice and Asgaya, who was training her, to contact all the officers and have them report to the briefing room in one hour. He then made his way to the room to check out the disc and see what route changes they would be making along the way. He loaded the disc and brought the data up on the screen, first they were to travel too Ertollos, then change their route and head to Lelkegain, and the third change would be to Spiria once there they will land at the base and meet with Admiral Madison who will be in charge of their weapons training.

After an hour all the officers entered the briefing room, Caalin had them take their seats and went over every detail of the mission, letting them know this was a training mission but they would still need to be on their toes because of the reports of pirate activity. Before everyone left the briefing room he said, "We are departing at 04:00 tomorrow so prepare your people for departure, we will a need twenty four hour watch during this mission because of the reported pirate activity, and because we will only be traveling at warp speed."

During lunch Caalin set with Ang, Ssam, Keyan, Clair and Jason and they were discussing the training for the girls while in route. Caalin turned to Ssam first, "Ok for tomorrow morning I want Aethia with Evalon on navigation, let Aethia handle everything unless Evalon see something wrong, then when we get to Ertollos we switch and Mari will be with Mylae doing the same thing as Evalon. For the third change I want both Aethia and Mylae working together checking and double checking each other." Ssam nodded, "That sounds like a good plan it will build confidence in their abilities." He looked over to Keyan, "We do the same with your girls Asgaya will be with Elice first leg and Astra will be with Takaria the second, and then the two girls will be together by their selves the last leg." Keyan smiled, "I will take care of the assignments."

Caalin then said, "The rest of us will stay on alert should any pirate activity be reported in the area." He then smiled, "We do have enough fighters now for our entire fighter team and Mouse is installing the stealth generators on them today, so we should be ready for almost anything." After that the group spent the rest of the time talking about other things and enjoying their meal.

After lunch Caalin made his way down to the shuttle bay to see if he could assist Mouse with anything, and when he got there Mouse and Sisten were just finish a picnic lunch Sisten had brought down for him. Caalin walked up to them, "I am sorry if I interrupted your picnic I can come back later." Sisten smiled, "No we had just finish, and I knew if I did not bring him something to eat he would have worked all day without eating." Caalin smiled at her, "Thank you for watching out for him, because I know you are right about that he doesn't know when to stop."

He then turned to Mouse, "I came down to see if I could help in anyway." Mouse spoke up, "Well I have finished with those two and just have these two before they all will be done." Caalin took off his outer shirt and was just wearing his tee shirt, "Well if you do the one you're standing by I will put the generator in the other one and we will be done in no time." Mouse looked over at him, "Are you sure you know what you are doing, I don't have a schematic diagram to give you." Caalin laughed, "Are you forgetting I built my on sky racer." Mouse grinned, "Ok you take care of that one and I will just check your work afterwards."

Sisten laughed, "You two are something else, and I don't know how Ang and Ssophia kept you straight back at Boldoron." Caalin grinned, "We walked around with a lot of bruises back then." Mouse jumped back in, "Yeah they did smack us a lot." Sisten walked off laughing as hard as she could finally shouting back to Mouse, "I will see you at dinner, please clean up before then." Caalin yelled back, "I'll make sure he does if I have to take a fire hose to him."

About two hours later the two of them had the last two fighters up and working, Caalin looked over at Mouse, "It looks like we both need to go get cleaned up now, we are filthy." Mouse looked at his arms and clothes, "I guess you are right I better hit the shower and get cleaned up before dinner." The two of them then headed off to their rooms to get cleaned up and change their uniforms. Then after they were cleaned and in fresh uniforms they made their way to the dining hall to meet Ang and Sisten.

After dinner Caalin walked Ang back to her room and kissed her good night then made his way back to his room to get some rest, 04:00 would be there sooner that he would want it to be. Before he made his way to his bedroom, he set down at the computer and pulled up the route they were taking to get an idea of places they could be ambushed if the pirates decided to attack, he wanted to be prepared for anything. Finally he shut the computer down and made his way to bed.

# CHAPTER 29

||||||||||||||||||||||||||||||||||||||||||||||

# AN UNEXPECTED FIGHT

At 03:00 Caalin was in the dining hall having breakfast where he saw Evalon, Mylae, Asgaya and Elice all having breakfast together before heading to the bridge. Dargon walked over and joined Caalin, "Well it looks like the navigation and communications teams for the first leg of our trip are up and ready to head out." Caalin smiled, "Yes it is nice to see those girls taking their training seriously, they would make great crew members for any ship should they decide that is what they want to do."

After a few minutes, Jon joined the two for breakfast and Caalin asked, "Are you handling engineering this morning?" Jon nodded, "Yes, but I just ran into Mouse already and he was on his way to the shuttle bay to double check the work on the new fighters." Dargon just shook his head, "Mouse is great at engineering, but he checks, double checks and sometimes triple checks his work." Caalin laughed, "That is probably why he is so good at what he does, it's because he is a perfectionist."

After breakfast Caalin and Dargon made their way to the bridge and Jon went to engineering, and the four girls were already at their stations doing checks. Caalin turned to Mylae, "All we all set to leave?" Mylae smiled, "Our course has been plotted and I am just waiting on your command to pull out of the docking port." Caalin then turned to Elice, "Contact the control center and ask for permission to undock and leave the port." Elice replied, "Yes captain." She then contacted the control center, got the permission and turned back to Caalin, "Permission has been granted, we can pull out when ready."

Caalin smiled, "Take us out slow and once we are clear of incoming and outgoing traffic take us to warp speed." Mylae took the ship out slowly up through the atmosphere and into space, after they were around one hundred kilometers out they went to warp speed. She then turned to Caalin, "We should reach Ertollos in eighteen hours at our current speed." Caalin smile, "Great maintain our course and speed and let me know if anything changes I am heading down to the shuttle bay if you need me."

Caalin made his way down to the shuttle bay where he found Mouse moving from fighter to fighter checking all the connections to make sure they were secure and correct. He walked over, "Mouse how many times are you going to check the fighters?" Mouse did not look up from what he was doing, "Until I am one hundred percent certain that they will not fail on any of your fighter team." Caalin replied, "Well I am one hundred and ten percent certain that they are done correctly, I know the engineer that worked on them did his job correctly the first time." Mouse dropped down from the last fighter, "I thank you for your vote of confidence, but I would not be able to live with myself if any one got injured or killed because I missed something." Caalin put his hand on Mouse's shoulder. "If that happed in would not be because of your work, it would be because of human error."

Caalin stood there looking at the fighters, "It is a shame that we have to drop out of stealth mode to fire our guns, that give the enemy a chance to target us, the best that we can do is drop from stealth, fire, then go back to stealth mode and the worst part is we are vulnerable when we do it." Mouse looked over at Caalin, "I know that is the biggest flaw in the system, but I am researching things to see if there are any changes I can make to correct that." Caalin laughed, "I figured you were already looking at the issue, just let me know if you come up with an answer and I will make sure you get all the help you need to carry out any changes you need to make."

The day went by quickly and quietly, Caalin had both lunch and dinner with Ang and soon it was nearing 22:00 and they were nearing Ertollos. Caalin made his way to the bridge and informed navigation to put them in orbit around the planet for the evening and they would leave for the second part of their journey the next morning at 04:00 again.

Tealana took over navigation for the evening and Keyan took over communications and Caalin let them both know to go to stealth and contact him if anything came up they could not handle. He then set there for another thirty minutes watching as they slowly orbited Ertollos, then he told the two good night and went to his room for a little sleep.

The next morning Caalin had eaten breakfast and was back on the bridge at 04:00 where he had Aethia plot the course to Lelkegain and take them away from Ertollos at warp speed. Takaria set quietly while monitoring communications for any incoming messages. Aethia turned to Caalin, "We should be arriving at Lelkegain in four hours." Caalin stood up, "That sounds great, contact me if anything come up; I am going to make my rounds through the ship."

Caalin left the bridge and walked back to the dining room to have a cup of tea before strolling through the rest of the ship. He was sipping on the tea when Takaria sent out a ship wide communications for him to return to the bridge they have an emergency distress call. Caalin leaped from his seat and ran back to the bridge, "What is the distress call for?" Aethia told him, "The passenger ship Abeona is being attacked by pirates and need emergency assistance and we are the closes ship to them." Caalin turned, "Contact the fighter team and have them meet me in the shuttle bay, contact Captain Anderson I need her to take over command here, and take us to warp four that should get us there in less than an hour."

Caalin took off toward the shuttle bay and as he did he passed Jean on the way, "I need you to take command of the ship we are about to engage pirates, go to stealth and wait for me to let you know what I need you to do." Jean replied, "OK, but you and your team be careful out there." Caalin shouted back, "We will do our best."

Caalin reach the shuttle bay and brought up the location where the passenger ship was being attack, there was one of the moons of Lelkegain near the site so Caalin contacted Jean, "Have the Seeker take a position with the moon between them and the battle." He then addressed his team, "We will go out in stealth mode, Dargon, Clair and Jason take the port side of the pirate ship, Faelara, Ric and Ssam take the starboard side. Rostrik and I will go for the engines then break off with Rostrik going below the ship and I will go over the top. We will have to come out of stealth to make our run, but once you have completed your run make sure you go back into stealth mode as you pull away, that way they will not know which way you are going before you hit them again. We will keep hitting them until we disable their engines and every gun on their ship."

As they were getting ready to leave the ship he informed Jean, "Keep the Seeker out of sight and safe, you are our backup should we need it." The Seeker came out of stealth mode and dropped the shields just long enough for the fighters to depart and once they were away from the ship the Seeker brought the shields back up and went stealth again. Caalin informed his team to turn their beacons on so they knew where each fighter was when they were in stealth mode. As they came around the moon they could see the passenger ship trying to hold its own against the pirates but its shields were giving away so Caalin gave the command, "Let's take the battle to the pirates, everyone go for the guns while Rostrik and I take out the engines."

Caalin led the charge with Rostrik right behind him; Dargon, Clair and Jason broke off and went for the guns along the port side of the pirate ship while Faelara, Ric and Ssam went for the starboard side. Caalin and Rostrik pounded the engines as they flew by taking them out with no problem, then Rostrik went below the ship taking out all the lower guns while Caalin did the same above the ship. Caalin then gave the command to hit the pirates one more time making sure no guns were left working.

The battle lasted less than twenty minutes and the pirate ship was now floating quietly with no power. Caalin contacted the pirate ship and warn them should they try to use their escape pods or shuttles to flee the area they would be taken out with no mercy. He then contacted Jean to bring the Seeker around to show they were not alone and as she did the Seeker came out of stealth mode right behind the pirate ship with all guns locked on.

Caalin contacted the passenger ship and asked if everything was ok, but the commander of the Abeona came back saying they had some damage to their jump engine and did not have the parts they needed to repair it. Caalin then asked permission to land his fighter on the Abeona and the commander came back telling him to us shuttle bay four they would light it up for him. Caalin saw the lights and took his fighter in bringing it to a soft landing in their shuttle bay.

Once on board Caalin was met by the first mate of the ship and Caalin asked to be taken to engineering to find out what parts they needed, he would then contact his ship and have the parts brought over to repair their jump drive. The first mate led him to engineering and introduced him to their chief engineer and Caalin quickly asked if he could give him a list of the parts they would need to get the jump drive back up and working. Within a minute their chief engineer had the listed and Caalin contacted Mouse on the Seeker to bring the needed parts over and assist with the repairs.

Within twenty minutes Mouse had gathered the parts and made his way over to the Abeona and was landing in the shuttle bay. He was met by the engineering team and they helped him with the parts and led him to engineering where he quickly began assisting with the repairs.

While Mouse was assisting in engineering the first mate took Caalin up to the bridge to meet with the Commander of the Abeona. As they walked onto the bridge the first mate spoke, "Commander Cavaltman may I introduce Captain Caalin Matthews the Commander of the Alliance Ship Seeker that came to our rescue." The Commander reached out his hand to shake Caalin's, "Well young Prince Matthews it is a pleasure to meet you, I know your father Lord Matthews very well, and I was surprised to find out his son is not only the youngest commander of an Alliance ship, but was the one that won the winnable battle that gave Alliance cadets difficulty for years."

Caalin looked puzzled, "Commander did my father tell you all that information?" The Commander laughed, "No lad, I have not seen your father in a couple of years, but you do have a couple of admirers that filled me in on all the information once they found out what ship saved us from the pirate." At that very moment Caalin heard two familiar voices from behind him speak in unison, "Well if it isn't Caalin Matthews once again our hero." Caalin slowly turned around and to his surprise there stood both Nesara Serinora and Deeleanna Teletora. He cleared his throat, "Sara, Dee what are the two of you doing on board the Abeona?" Dee spoke up, "We were on our way to Spiria when we were attacked. We made a stop a Lelkegain to drop off some passengers and were attacked before the ship could jump."

The Commander then spoke, "Yes we were taking them to Spiria, but because of the pirate attack we have been called back to our home port by the company, they want to assess the damage and make some modifications so the girls will be late for their new jobs." Caalin looked over to the two girls, "New jobs, you girls no longer work for the headmaster?" Sara shook her head, "No he got called to work at the Alliance Headquarters and was on his way there when we left Boldoron, and we have jobs at the military base on Spiria working for Admiral Madison."

Caalin thought for a moment, "Well you are in luck we are on our way to Spiria to meet with Admiral Madison for weapons training and if you would like we could transport you there." The two girls smiled at each other then Dee said, "That would be great we will get to see some of our old friends from school." Caalin turned to the Commander, "Sir if you can have their gear transferred to our shuttle in your shuttle bay I will have my Engineering Officer transport them to the Seeker." Caalin then turned to Dee and Sara, "Mouse is here helping their engineers with their jump drive and he will fly you over to the Seeker, I will stop by engineering to let him know you are coming with him, and then I need to take my fighter back over to the ship so I will see you ladies later when you get on board."

Dee and Sara left to go pack their gear and before Caalin could leave the Commander stopped him long enough to thank him once again for saving his ship. Caalin smiled, "Sir it was our honor to assist you in your time in need, we have contacted the Alliance and will stay until they have ships here to take care of the pirate ship and its crew." Caalin then left to make his way back down to engineering and prepare Mouse for the shock of Dee and Sara coming back to the Seeker with him.

Once in engineering Mouse could not believe it when he told him about Dee and Sara, plus the fact that they were going to the same place the Seeker was heading. Mouse then made the obvious statement that had been on Caalin's mind since he saw Dee and Sara, "Well you may want to head back to the ship to prepare Ang for the two new guests that will be traveling with us to Spiria." Caalin lowered his head, "You are right and I don't know how she is going to like it, they were not her favorite staff members back at Boldoron." Mouse slapped him on the shoulder, "I am just glad I am not in your shoes, but you had better head out and do it as soon as possible; I am about done here."

Caalin left Mouse finishing the work he was doing and went down and boarded his fighter. The rest of the fighter team was still on standby around the pirate ship waiting for further orders, as Caalin left the Abeona he told the fighters to keep an eye on the pirate ship until the Alliance cruisers arrive to take over he was heading back to the ship to prepare for two new guests that will be traveling with them to Spiria."

# CHAPTER 30

## ON TO SPIRIA

Once back on the Seeker Caalin made his way toward the bridge stopping by medical to talk to Ang. As he walked in Ang walked over to greet him, "Did everything go well for everyone?" Caalin nodded, "Yes we disabled the pirate ship and have called for Alliance backup to take over with the prisoners, but when I visited with the Commander of the Abeona I found that they were transporting two people we know to Spiria and since his ship has been called back to their home port he has asked that since we are heading to Spiria could we take the two passengers with us."

Ang gave Caalin a look, "I know you, so I know you told him we would am I correct?" Caalin nodded, "Yes I told him we would take them with us, and Mouse is bringing them over on the shuttle once he has finished with assisting their engineers." Ang smiled, "Great we will get rooms ready for them, but who are the individuals?" By this time Ssophia and Sisten had joined them and Ssophia jumped in, "Yes Mr. Matthews who are our guest going to be?" Caalin looked down knowing that Ang was not going to be thrilled, "Dee and Sara are the two individuals we will be transporting to Spiria they both have jobs working for Admiral Madison."

There was an awkward silence then Ang spoke, "That is great, we haven't seen them since we left the school so it will be good to catch up on what has been happening back there." Ssophia jumped in, "Well we had better get them some rooms ready they may want to get cleaned up when they arrive." Caalin breathed a sigh of relief, "Thanks girls for not making it any more awkward than what it was." Ang reach over an took his hand, "I know how sweet you are and you would not have left them to find another way there, and besides this will give us time to catch up on things." She then turned to the other two girls as she was walking out, "Let's go get their rooms ready." Ssophia paused as she walked by Caalin, "It seems Ang is going to let Dee and Sara know where she stands when it comes to you so I think you are safe as long as you don't do anything stupid."

Caalin just lowered and shook his head, "Well I need to get to the bridge and relieve Jean." He turned and made his way up to the bridge where he thanked Jean for taking over command and telling her he would take it from there. Jean smile, "You are welcome, but I just got a communications from Mouse that he is headed back with two guests, Sara and Dee, this is going to be an interesting trip to Spiria." Caalin looked over at her, "Please don't you start in on me I have already gotten an ear full from Ssophia." Jean left the bridge laughing, "Don't worry it will all be fine."

A few minutes later Mouse had landed the shuttle back in the shuttle bay and was escorting both Dee and Sara toward the living quarters. As they made their way across the shuttle bay Ang, Ssophia and Sisten were there to greet them. Ang walked over and gave each of them a hug, "It is great to see the two of you again we have rooms ready for you." She then turned to Marty, "Can you have your crew make sure their luggage gets to their rooms I have already sent the information to your system." Marty smiled, "I will take care of it right away."

As Ang was leading them to their rooms Dee spoke up, "Ang I hear Caalin finally got around to making it official and you and he are boyfriend and girl friend, Sara and I are so happy for the two of you. I know you didn't like the way we use to act around him, but we couldn't help it he is so handsome and charming, but you don't have to worry about us anymore we know where we stand with him, we are all just friends." Ang turn and gave them both another hug, "Thank you I needed to hear that, I didn't know how to feel about us all being on the same ship together." Sara smiled, "Don't worry Caalin made his decision and it was a good one the two of you make a wonderful couple."

Caalin was back on the bridge when he got a communications from Alliance Headquarters stating that three cruisers should arrive within an hour to take control over the pirate ship and its crew. Caalin then contacted his fighter team and gave them the information telling them that once the Alliance cruisers take over they are to return to the Seeker.

He then turned to Aethia, "Once all the fighters have returned to the ship put us in orbit around Lelkegain we will leave for Spiria tomorrow morning." Caalin then walked out and to the dining hall to talk with Belrion and Tehaena about something special. Once in the dining hall the three of them sat down for some tea and Caalin discussed what his plan was, "I think we need to through a party to celebrate our defeat of the pirates and the saving of the Abeona. My fighter squad did a great job and I think they deserve a celebration." Tehaena smiled, "I think that is a wonderful idea, it would show them how proud we are of them and boost their moral at the same time; we will get right on it." With that the two of them jumped up and ran back into the kitchen to get started, and Caalin made his way back to the bridge.

When Caalin arrive back on the bridge he received a communications from Commander Cavaltman of the Abeona thanking him for all the help with the pirates and getting their jump engine back online, and with that the Abeona made a jump and disappeared. Minutes later three Alliance cruisers appeared and the commander in charge thanked Caalin and his crew for their great work and informed him that they would take over from there so they were free to withdraw. Caalin called his fighters back and informed them once they had secured their fighters to get cleaned up and wait for further orders.

Ninety minutes went by then Caalin turned to the people on the bridge, "Go to stealth mode, turned all the sensors on to monitor the area around us up to a thousand kilometers and make your way to the dining hall." He then sent out a ship wide communications, "Everyone secure your stations and make your way to the dining hall I will meet you there." Marty put the androids in charge of handling thing on the cargo deck and he and his team made their way toward the dining hall. Ang, Ssophia and Sisten led Dee and Sara to the dining hall while the rest of the crew made their way up as well. Once everyone was in the dining hall standing around to see what Caalin had to say he stood up on a chair, "Thank you all for making it, I would like you all to know that everyone did a great job today and I am very proud of all of you, with that said we are celebrating a job well done so eat up and enjoy, then get plenty of rest tonight we leave for Spiria tomorrow at 07:00."

Dargon made his way over to Caalin, "Why such a later start in the morning we usually depart around 04:00." Caalin put his hand on Dargon's shoulder, "I want everyone to be rested up when we arrive at

Spiria I don't know what Admiral Madison has in store for us." Dargon just nodded, "I guess you have to plan ahead and you seem to always be one step ahead on your plans." Caalin laughed, "I just err on the side of caution." Dargon walked away to join Mari and the two of them set down at one of the corner tables to enjoy their meal together.

Sara and Dee were setting with Ang, Ssophia and Gahe telling them all the stories they had heard about the Seeker and its crew when Caalin joined them. Ssophia looked over at him, "Well it is nice for the heroic captain of the Alliance Ship Seeker to grace us with his presents." Caalin looked perplexed when Ang took his hand, "Have a seat and we will fill you in on everything." She then turned to Ssophia, "Now stop with your teasing this is supposed to be a calibration not a tease feast." Ssophia lowered her head, "I know, but I just couldn't help myself it was just too easy." Gahe broke out laughing, "Ang I can't believe you stopped her in her tracks, I have never been able to do that." Ssophia elbowed him in the ribs, "And you will never be able to Mr. Gluskap."

Caalin took his seat and everyone began filling him in on all the stories that were going around about the Seeker and its captain. Caalin looked over at Dee and Sara, "You can't believe everything you hear about us, some of those stories were greatly exaggerated." Dee then asked, "Was there any truth in any of the stories?" Ssophia smiled, "There was truth in all of them but there was also some exaggeration in there as well." Then she and Ang began correcting all the stories they heard.

The party went on for a few hours then everyone began making it out of the dining hall and off to their rooms to get some rest. Caalin walked Ang to her room and told her, "I am glad to see that you are getting along well with Dee and Sara." Ang kissed him, "It is easy now that they know that you are all mine." Caalin told her good night and made his way back to the bridge where he took his seat and stared out into space for a couple of hours wondering what Spiria had in store for them.

The next morning Caalin had his breakfast and was on the bridge by 06:30 and a few minutes later the rest of the crew appeared to join him. At 07:00 he turned to Aethia and Mylae, "Set our course for Spiria and take us out at warp four, that should get us there in four hours." He then turned to Elice and Takaria, "Contact Spiria and let them know our estimated time of arrival and find out what port they would like us to land at." They were off and within minutes Elice let him know they would be landing at Alliance Base Twelve in the northwest hemisphere at port C-Twelve.

Four hours later they had received their landing clearance and were making their way down through the atmosphere and landing at port C-Twelve. Once on the ground the ground crew began securing the landing couplings and a representative was requesting permission to come onboard. Caalin granted permission and the representative boarded the ship and made his way to the bridge. The representative informed Caalin that he had a meeting with Admiral Madison at 17:00, a crewman will pick him up at 16:30 and arrangements had been made for Dee and Sara to be picked up at 15:00. After that the representative left the ship and Caalin had Takaria contact Dee and Sara to meet him for lunch and he then left the bridge and made his way to medical to ask Ang to join them.

# CHAPTER 31

||||||||||||||||||||||||||||||||||||||||||||

## MEETING WITH
## ADMIRAL MADISON

During lunch Caalin informed Dee and Sara about what the
representative had said about them being picked up at 15:00 and asked
if they had everything packed and ready to leave. Dee informed him
that they never unpacked any of their things so it would not take them
long to be ready to disembark the ship. The rest of the meal the girls
talked among themselves so Caalin just finished his meal and excused
himself to head back to the bridge. After lunch the girls made their
way down to see Marjorie who was in the workout room with Arria
and Phyla doing hand to hand combat training. Marjorie paused their
training long enough to speak with the girls and give Arria and Phyla
time to cool down. After their short conversation Dee and Sara went to
get their luggage together for Marty's team to take down to the dock.

It was now 14:45 and Ang, Ssophia, Dee and Sara stopped by the bridge
to let Caalin know that they were departing and that they hoped to see
everyone again before they leave the planet. Caalin wished them well
in their new jobs and stated that they would do their best to make sure
they come by to see them before departing the planet. Dee and Sara
made their way down to the dock where a crewmember was waiting to

escort them to their new living quarters; he informed them that they would be escorted to their new office the next morning.

Caalin made it a point to go to the dining hall for something to eat before he departed for his meeting and at 16:45 he made his way off the ship and down to the dock. Once he reached the dock a young ensign was there to meet him with a salute, "Captain Matthews I am here to escort you to Admiral Madison's office, I am Ensign Reynolds." Caalin returned his salute, "Ensign do not worry about formalities with me I am okay with you just calling me Caalin when it is just the two of us otherwise just Captain Matthews will be fine." The Ensign nodded, "I think I should just call you Captain Matthews then sir." Caalin just smiled, "If that is your choose then I am fine with it."

The Ensign led him to a hover car and once they were on board they left the docking area and drove across the base to the Admiral's Office. He then escorted Caalin up to the office and once there the receptionist took over and escorted him in to see the Admiral. Once inside the Admiral not looking up from the papers he was reading, "Have a seat Captain Matthews I will be with you once I finish this paper work." Caalin took a seat and stared at the Admiral who was an older white haired man with a clean cut beards and steal blue eyes. The Admiral finished reading the papers then signed them and handed them off to his receptionist to take care of the rest. The Admiral stood up and walked around the desk reaching out his hand to shake Caalin's. Caalin quickly stood up and offer his hand for the hand shake. The Admiral had a big smile on his face, "Well lad it is a great day for me, I finally get to meet the grandson of my old friend Julius Horatio Matthews, your grandfather would not stop talking about you from the time you were born up until the time we lost him in the final battle with the Red Dragons in the Vodyaron Star System. Your Grandfather was a great man and it seems that his grandson is making a name for himself as well."

Caalin lowered his head, "Well Admiral I will agree my grandfather was outstanding, but I am not my grandfather and will never be as great an officer as he was." The Admiral making his way back around his desk and taking his seat, "I beg to differ with you lad, I have read all the reports on everything you have accomplished and I have to say you are your grandfathers grandson by all counts." Caalin taking his seat, "Sir everything I accomplished was because of the friends that are my crew and supporters, I could not have done any of that on my own." The Admiral looked straight into Caalin's eyes, "I beg to differ lad, there are a lot of things you did on your own mainly for the sake of those around you and those things you cannot deny."

The Admiral then cleared his throat, "Well let's get to the real reason you and your crew is here, it is for weapons training. Tomorrow afternoon we will have transportation waiting at the docks to transport your entire crew to our weapons training facility on the other side of the planet. While you are going through your training we will be upgrading the Seeker with new weapons, upgrading the engines and installing new software for scanning, tracking and targeting. You need to make sure everyone has all their gear and equipment and are on the dock at 13:00 tomorrow." Caalin asked, "Can you tell me what type of training we will be getting?" The Admiral smiled, "Your crew will get complete combat training, and not only weapon's qualification but urban assault training and you will also compete against one of my teams in capture the flag. Now I think you need to get back to the Seeker to prepare your crew and by crew I mean everyone onboard the Seeker."

The Admiral stood up and called for the ensign and when he arrive the Admiral smiled, "Take Captain Matthews back to his ship he has to brief his crew and prepare for their training to begin." The ensign escorted Caalin back to the hover car and drove him back to the dock where the Seeker set, "Well sir good luck with your training it is going to be tough." Caalin thanked him for the ride then turned and made his way back on board the ship, once on board he made his way to the bridge. When he arrived on the bridge Dargon was setting in the command chair and Caalin turned to Astra, "Contact everyone onboard and have them meet me in the dining hall immediately I have information I need to share and everyone needs to be there including everyone on the bridge."

Caalin then turned to Dargon, "let's make our way to the dining hall I need to talk to the kitchen staff as well and Astra once you are done come join us." Once in the dining hall Caalin went to the kitchen and told Belrion that his team would need to be at the meeting with the rest of the crew. Fifteen minutes later everyone onboard the Seeker was setting in the dining hall waiting to hear what Caalin needed to tell them. Caalin stood up on a chair so everyone could see him, he looked around the room and everyone got quite, "Ok I need to let everyone know tomorrow at 13:00 everyone on the Seeker will need to be on the dock with all your gear to meet the transportation that will be taking us to the training facility for combat weapons training, no one will remain on the Seeker." He then turned to Clair, "I need your team to make sure the weapon have been place into storage units for transportation as well. While we are going through our training the maintenance team here will be installing new equipment and upgrading other systems."

Dargon started to ask a question but before he could Caalin said, "That is all the information I have the Admiral would not tell me anything else so it is just as much a surprise to me as it is to all of you." He then dismissed everyone to go began preparing to leave the ship and turned to Belrion, "Is your team going to have any problems being ready by 13:00?" Belrion replied, "No but we will have to stop serving meals by 10:00 in order to have the kitchen cleaned before we depart." Caalin nodded, "That will not be a problem but let me know if you need any help and I will get some volunteers to assist you."

Caalin made his way to his room and packed his bags then walked down to the shuttle bay and stood there staring at the fighters. Ang walked up behind him, "I thought this was where you were heading when you walked right past me without saying a word." Caalin jumped, "I'm sorry my mind was elsewhere." Ang took his hand, "What is bothering you I can see it in your eyes." Caalin looked at her, "I don't know how tough this training is going to be and I am worried that some of the crew may recent me for getting them involve in it, especially Arria, Phyla, Mylae, Aethia, Elice and Takaria they are just our guest and not actual crew members and I don't know how they feel about this." There was a voice from behind them, "We are fine with it Caalin so stop worrying." Ang and Caalin turned and there were all six of the girls and it was Arria doing the talking. Arria smile, "We didn't mean to intrude but Elice spotted you when you walked by Ang without seeing her so she came to talk to the rest of us. She thought you were worrying about how we felt about being included in the training." Elice then spoke up, "Well Captain Matthews you need to know the way everyone onboard has treated us since you saved us has made us feel like we were part of the crew. In fact we all decided that when we return to Alliance Headquarters we are all going to join the Alliance and request to become part of your crew." Arria laughed at the look on

Caalin's face, "What she is trying to tell you is to stop worrying we are happy to be included."

Ang reached over and wiped a tear from Caalin's face, "Ship Commanders are not suppose to cry." Caalin looked at her with a big smile, "Whose crying those were tears of joy." The girls all ran over and gave Caalin hugs and thanked him for worrying about them. Caalin cleared his throat, "I am more than happy that you ladies want to become part of our family and I will do everything in my power to make it happen for you, now don't you think you need to get your things packed for tomorrow." They all laughed as they left to go pack their bags for the next day leaving Ang and Caalin in the shuttle bay. Ang then leaned over and kissed Caalin on the cheek, "See there you were worried for nothing, those girls are part of this crew and want to be treated that way, and that is because you are a great Captain."

Caalin then looked at Ang, "Well we had better go get some sleep we have a big day tomorrow." Ang took his arm, "Only if you walk me back to my room." Caalin smiled, "It will be my pleasure." He escorted her back to her room, gave her a kiss and then went straight to his room.

# CHAPTER 32

||||||||||||||||||||||||||||||||||||||||||||

# NEW CREWMEMBERS AND MOUSE'S NEW SKILL

The next morning Caalin was up early and made his way to breakfast thinking about what Arria and Elice had told him the night before, then after breakfast he went straight to the bridge. When he reached the bridge Mari was there checking messages on the communication system. Caalin turned to her, "Mari can you contact Councilman Moreland for me I need to speak with him before we leave the ship." Mari smile, "I will contact his office right away." She sent the communications and within five minutes turned back to Caalin, "Councilman Moreland will contact you in one hour, do you want to take his call in the briefing room?" Caalin smiles, "That would be great, I am going to head back to the dining hall and get some tea then go straight to the briefing room and you can transfer the call to me when it comes in." Mari let him know she would take care of it and he left to walk back to the dining hall for tea.

After getting his tea Caalin made his way to the briefing room to await the call and while he was setting there he went over what he wanted to discuss with the Councilman. Soon the call came through from Councilman Moreland, "Captain Matthews how are you doing lad?" Caalin replied, "I am doing great sir, I hope you are as well." The Councilman laughed, "As well as I can be, now let me guess why you called is it because the six young ladies that your crew saved wishing to stay on board the Seeker and become part of your crew and you need uniforms for them?" Caalin had a look of shock on his face and the Councilman continued, "Don't look surprised it seem your young Lieutenant Avora sent me a message late last night and I have had my people scrabbling to get the uniforms altered for the young ladies. You should have their uniforms within the next hour they went out earlier this morning and the ship should be there soon, and before you ask she also sent along their measurements so the uniforms will fit them all perfectly we were just waiting for the word that they wanted to join your crew."

Caalin scratched his head, "How were you certain they would join my crew?" The Councilman laughed, "Young man whether you know it or not you have a way of drawing people to you that want to help you with whatever you are doing. I could not believe it when Nathaniel Keayan told me about it, but I have seen it myself and know for a fact it is true. You are a natural leader and everyone around you wants to be a part of your endeavors, you make this old man as proud of you as your father and Nathaniel."

The intercom buzzed and Councilman Moreland smile, "You had better answer that lad; I think the uniforms have arrived and you need to get them to the ladies, we can talk again after all your training is over." Caalin just stood up, "Thank you for being one step ahead of me Councilman I will talk to you once Admiral Madison is done with us." Before the councilman signed off he told Caalin to do his best and take care of his crew. Caalin smiled, "You did not have to tell me that sir, I have the best crew around and I will do my best to take care of them all."

Caalin left the briefing room and quickly made his way down to the cargo bay where Marti and his team were receiving the shipment containers. As he walked up Marti turned, "Caalin we just received these containers for our six guest should I have them delivered to their rooms." Caalin nodded, "Yes please as soon as possible they will need them right away." Marti replied, "We will take them now."

Caalin then left to find Ang and as he made his way up to the medical facility she was on her way down. Caalin looked at her, "You are always one step ahead of me; you sent a message to the councilman last night about the girl's uniforms." Ang gave Caalin a, I don't know what you are talking about look, and then broke into laughter, "Well I knew you would want to get them their uniforms, and I didn't want you to worry about them getting here in time." Caalin smiled, "Thank you for doing that, the uniforms have just arrive and Marti's team is delivering them as we speak." Ang hugged him, "Great I will go and let Ssophia and Sisten know and we will see if we can help them with their uniforms." She turned and went back up the steps leaving Caalin standing there shaking his head and thinking, *"I don't know how she keeps reading my mind."*

The morning flew by fast and by 12:00 everyone had their luggage on the dock to be transported to the training facility. Caalin made one last walk through the ship before joining everyone on the dock and when he arrived he was pleasantly surprise about how good the girls looked in their uniforms. Ang walked over to him, "They look good don't they?" Caalin smiled, "They are going to make a good addition to the crew and the uniforms look great on them, so thank you again for your help." Ang gave him a peck on the cheek, "My pleasure Mr. Matthews."

After a few minutes Dee and Sara showed up and made their way over to Caalin and Ang, "We are here to escort your crew to the training facility we have the transport shuttle on the other side of the docking port, and don't worry about your bags they will be taken straight there, your crew will be given a little tour of the training area on the way." Caalin and the crew followed the two girls across the dock to the other side where a large shuttle awaited them. Everyone boarded, took their seats and the shuttle doors slowly closed, then the shuttle lifted off the ground made a turn and moved westward.

There was a large screen in the front of the shuttle that showed them what they were flying over and while they were doing so Dee was explaining what they were seeing. After a short time they crossed over a large body of water and then a large island and Dee spoke up "This is the training Island and it is exactly 50,532 square kilometers of mountain, rivers, valleys and flat land. To the north of the facility is the firing ranges, to the south are the urban assault area and to the west is the capture the flag combat area. Not everyone will participate in urban assault or the capture the flag competition as that will be based on how you perform in the other areas, just remember this is not to make combat soldiers out of all of you but to make you proficient in handling the weapons should you need to."

The shuttle then came to a landing near a large building at the far end of what looked like a military base and that is when Dee said, "This building is where you will be staying while you are doing your training, your names should be on the door of your rooms and all your luggage should already be there so go ahead and get squared away and we will be back later to take you to dinner and to meet Admiral Madison." Everyone departed the shuttle and made their way inside to find their rooms and unpack their clothes.

Everyone made it to their rooms and when Mouse got to his the first thing he did after unpacking his uniforms and hanging them up was to unpack a spare arm that he had been working on in private. Mouse had scanned the arm that he had been given by Matthew when they jumped to the future and decided to build one of his own but with some improvements. Mouse laid the arm on the table in his room and opened its maintenance compartment then opened another box and pull out two extremely small generators that he had miniaturized to fit inside the arm. He worked diligently for a couple of hours until he finally had the two installed and they were wired into the arm itself. He then removed the arm he was wearing and attached the new arm in its place and watched as the nanos covered it with synthetic skin.

Mouse stood up with a smile on his face, "Now for the big test." He walked over to a mirror on the wall and concentrated and within seconds he disappeared and then reappeared. Mouse was delighted his new arm worked great and he had successfully installed a force field generator and stealth generator in his mechanical arm and thanks to the nanos in his system he was able to control it, but he did not know if the shield would work or how large an area he could cover. He set down and thought for a moment, "I need to talk to Caalin about this and see if there is some place we can test it where no one will see us."

Mouse made his way out of his room and down the hall until he reached Caalin's room and knocked on the door. Caalin open the door, "Hey Mouse, come on in do you need me for something?" Mouse smiled, "I need to test my new arm." Caalin looked at Mouse then at his left arm, "I don't see anything different about your arm is that a new one?" Mouse replied, "Yes, I thought it would be better if I had a spare arm just in case something happened to the other one, but this one is better watch." Caalin watched and to his amazement Mouse vanished right in front of him." When Mouse reappeared he was standing right next to Caalin, "I install a shield generator and a stealth generator in this one, and it took me a long time to get them small enough to fit." Caalin patted Mouse on the back, "That is amazing, but what do you need my help with?" Mouse looked over at him, "I need to test the range that I can cover with the two generators and I want to keep it a secret as long as possible so I need a private place to test it and help determining the range." Caalin thought for a moment, "Let me talk with the Admiral and find out if there is a place where I can work with my crew out of sight of his personnel and get back to you." Mouse agreed and left Caalin's room heading back to his, he need to put his other arm in the case he took the new one out of then secure the case.

Later Sara and Dee returned and escorted the Seeker crew to a large dining hall two buildings down from theirs and Sara told them, "This is where you will be dining while you are on the base." Dee turned to Caalin, "Admiral Madison would like you to join him at his table up front." Caalin followed her and she escorted him to the table and the Admiral smiled at him, "Take a seat lad I will explain what your crews training will consist of while you are here." The moment Caalin set down food started being set around him and the Admiral explained, "I hope you don't mind but I went ahead and ordered for you I hope you enjoy the meal."

Caalin began to eat as the Admiral began explaining the training, "Your training will consist of five days beginning tomorrow with weapon familiarization and weapons qualification at twenty five meters, day two you will be moved back to fifty meters for qualification and day three you will move back to one hundred meters for qualifications." Caalin thought for a moment, "So three days of just qualifying with the weapon?" The Admiral replied, "Yes we want to make sure your crew can handle the weapons and hit what they are aiming at, on day four not all of your crew will go through the urban assault course you will select the personnel for that training. On the fifth day you will pick the personnel you want to participate in the capture the flag battle against my troops and you can pick as many people you want on your team up to twenty."

Caalin set quietly while eating and thinking, "I understand, but now I need to ask is there any place where my people can training and not be seen by any of your personnel? We want to go over tactics and also get some hand to hand training in as well." The Admiral perked up, "Oh I see you want to use Marjorie Kai to help your team to get ready for capture the flag, I think that is an excellent idea, so if you go down into the basement of the building you are staying in you will find a gymnasium that covers the entire length of the building and it has all the mats you need plus some other equipment you are free to use." Caalin replied, "Thank you sir I will check it out when we get back to the building, and I will inform my people of what the training will be." The Admiral began to stand up, "That is great lad now enjoy your meal, I am sorry I have other things to take care of but I will be monitoring the progress of your training."

After dinner Caalin and his crew made their way back to their domicile and Caalin called for the team leaders to meet him in the commons area for a quick briefing. Once everyone was there he went over everything the Admiral had told him about the training then looked over at Belrion and Tehaena, "Your group will only have to participate in the first three days for the weapons qualification and not the urban assault training or the capture the flag event." He then dismissed the group to get the information out to the rest of the crew, but as they were all leaving he grabbed Mouse, "Come with me we are going to check out the gym in the basement, it may be just the location to test your arm."

The two of them made their way down the flight of stairs to the basement and once they entered the room all the lights came on lighting up the huge room. Caalin looked around, "I think this room may be big enough to get some idea of how big a range your shield can cover." Mouse walked to the other side of the room and turned to Caalin, "Toss one of those balls over there at me and let's see how close it gets." Caalin walked to the other end of the room and picked up a ball then turned and tossed it, but it went about a meter before it hit something invisible and dropped to the floor." Caalin looked at Mouse, "Looks like you can at lease shield about thirty five meters, but it looks like to get an accurate distance we would need to do this outside."

Mouse thought for a moment, "Let's test the stealth, we can place those balls all around the room and see how far I can make them disappear." Caalin began tossing balls all around the room with some of them reaching the wall at the other end of the room, then once they were all scattered around Mouse made his way to the middle. Mouse stood in the middle of the room and thought for a moment then he, Caalin, all the balls and equipment around them plus three of the outside walls disappeared. The walls disappearing startle Mouse and everything quickly reappeared and he walked over to Caalin, "I think I can cover a lot more area than the room can handle so I think you are right and we should find a place outside to test it."

Caalin took a seat on a piece of equipment to think, "Well there is that huge landing area where we landed when we got here, but we need to do it at night so no one will see us. Meet me in the commons room at midnight and we can test it then." Mouse smiled, "I knew you would think of something." Caalin then stopped him, "I think we need some more people to help us so is it alright to bring Ang, Ssam and Ssophia with me?" Mouse laughed, "Of course I trust all of them to keep it a secret." The two of them went back upstairs and then to their rooms, Caalin stopped by Ang's room and asked her to get Ssophia and the two of them join him and Mouse at midnight in the commons room and he would explain things then. He then went to Ssam's room and told him about the midnight test explaining that it needed to remain a secret for now.

Later at midnight they all met in the commons room and when Mouse arrived Sisten was with him as he walked up he explained to everyone, "I trust Sisten with my secret so I brought her along." Caalin laughed, "We weren't questioning you we were just surprised." The six of them left the building and made their way to the landing area and Mouse walked to the center of the landing pad.

Caalin looked at the area and then turn to Ssam, "I figure this area is at least two hundred meters across and two hundred and fifty long do you agree?" Ssam looked over the area, "It has to be at least that." Caalin then told everyone, "Make a circle around Mouse with everyone about fifty meters away from him." Once everyone was in position he told Mouse to do his thing, and as soon as Mouse did everyone disappeared from sight." Caalin then told him that was enough and they all reappeared, and he then had everyone move out another fifty meters and repeated the experiment with the same results.

They continued the experiment until they reached the limit for Mouse's stealth abilities which seem to have hit its limit at around two hundred meters. Caalin walk over to Mouse that is great I just wish you were able to designate what you wanted to shield instead of shielding everything around you. Mouse thought for a moment, "I think I might be able to do that if I concentrate a little harder." He then asked the girls to move back out until they were at least one hundred and fifty meters away and he then asked Caalin and Ssam to stay at seventy five meters away. Mouse then looked around the area and concentrated then all of a sudden the girls disappeared but the boys were still visible.

Everyone then came back in and congratulated Mouse on his accomplishment and Caalin asked him how was he able to do it. Mouse replied, "I just had to picture it in my mind then I was able to apply the field wherever I wanted to." Caalin slapped Mouse on the back then told everyone, "Let's keep this a secret, this may come in handy during the capture the flag event." Mouse looked over at Caalin, "I don't know what you are cooking up in your head, but I'm all in for it because it has to be good." After that they all made it back to their rooms to get some sleep they would need it for weapon qualification.

# CHAPTER 33

||||||||||||||||||||||||||||||||||||||||||||||

# TACTICAL WEAPONS TRAINING

The next morning everyone was up and in the commons area when Caalin made his way down, "Well everyone our training begins today so let's all head over to the dining hall and have a good breakfast." Everyone made their way out the door and over to the dining hall for breakfast. Caalin was enjoying his meal when Sara came over, "Well Captain Matthews I am here to take you and your crew over to the firing range so when everyone is done we can leave." After a few minutes everyone had finished their meal and was waiting outside for Sara to take them over to the firing range.

She then came out and led everyone over and introduced them to Captain Galerian the instructor in charge of the range. Galerian explain to them that the first part of the morning would be just firing the weapons down range at the targets and getting familiar with how they handled. After lunch they all would be firing the weapons for scores to qualify with them and at the end of the three days the individual or individuals with an expert score would get their name on the plaque in the lobby of the administrative building. Everyone made their way onto the range and down the row standing behind one of the weapons that was setting on a table in front of them.

Captain Galerian spoke over the loud speaker, "At all times you will keep the barrel of the weapon pointed down range toward the target, if I see anyone doing something else I will have you pulled from the range." There was a pause then he continued, "Everyone pickup your weapon and when you fill comfortable begin firing on the targets trying to get as close to the bulls eye as possible." Everyone lifted the weapon and took aim then began firing on the targets. Caalin seemed to be a wizard at this as every shot he fire were direct hits on the bulls eye, while everyone else were having issues zeroing in their weapon to hit the bulls eye and some were even having problems hitting the target itself.

Caalin laid his weapon down after completely hollowing out the center of the target then he raised his hand for Captain Galerian to stop the firing. Galerian announced over the intercom to stop all firing, and once everyone had placed their weapons down he ask Caalin why he stop the firing. Caalin walked over to him, "Do you mind if I have a quick meeting with my crew, I think it will help them." Galerian nodded, "Go ahead, just let me know when we can continue, and you can come off the range I can see you already are a capable marksman at this distance."

Caalin called everyone to the entrance and had them all take a seat, then he began telling them all that they needed to relax, he smiled, "You all need to breath, before you fire your weapon take a breath then let it out slowly while you are taking aim, then fire by squeezing the trigger not jerking it." He then told them how to line up the sights to get a perfect shot, telling them, "slow down, and take three shots and see where you hit the target then you can adjust your aim accordingly." After that everyone made their way back out onto the range and once they were all in position Galerian gave them permission to continue firing."

Galerian was amazed that Caalin's little pep talk had helped as much as it did; everyone was now getting better and closer to hitting the bull's eye. Everyone except Caalin continued firing weapon until lunch then they took a break and made their way to the dining hall to eat. While at lunch people kept coming over and asking Caalin question after question about how to aim properly and about their breathing so he did not get a lot of time to enjoy his meal.

After lunch they made their way back to the range and took their places behind the weapons. Galerian explained the scoring for the qualification, "OK you will be firing five round at a time, the center of the target counts as twenty points, the next ring counts as ten points and the third ring counts as five, anything further out on the target does not count. We will be doing ten sets of five rounds each time, the highest score you could get per round is one hundred points and you will need a minimum of six hundred points to meet qualification as a marksman, seven hundred and fifty points qualifies you as a sharpshooter and nine hundred points or higher makes you an expert." Mouse spoke up, "What happens if you get a perfect score of one thousand points?" Galerian laughed, "Well that has never happened, but if it did you would be the supreme expert." Mouse shouted, "OK let's all go for the supreme expert qualification." Everyone cheered and one person shouted, "If anyone can do it Caalin can." Galerian looked over at Caalin, "Well Captain Matthews it looks like your crew has confidence in you so you can't let them down can you?" Caalin just smile, "Well, I will do my best."

Galerian gave the command, "Weapons down range, and with five rounds fire." Everyone fired their first five rounds with Caalin putting

206

all five of his in the center. This went on for the rest of the afternoon with Galerian giving the command and everyone firing and the scores being tallied as they went. By the end of the day Caalin had a perfect score of one thousand followed by Rostrik, Dargon, Ssam, Clair, Faelara, Resrassira,Aeron, Ekdrin and Jason scoring in the nine hundred. Everyone else scored above seven hundred except Belrion, Tehaena and the kitchen staff who still qualified in the six hundreds.

Galerian spoke, "Congratulation on doing so well today, but you will need to do as good or better for the next two days to be fully qualified, the next two days are more difficult as we move further back." He then released everyone for the rest of the day and they made their way back to their rooms to get cleaned up for dinner. On the way back Ssam asked Caalin how he managed to score so high because he was finding it difficult to keep his aim but Caalin made it look easy. Caalin just shook his head, "I don't know myself it just seems like my body knows where the shot is going to go and the more I concentrate on the target the more times I hit where I want it to hit."

Ang came over to Caalin, "You put on an impressive show today with your marksmanship are you going to do that well tomorrow?" Caalin laughed, "I should qualify but I am not sure if it will be a perfect score or not." Mouse and Ssam over heard Caalin's comment and Ssam jumped in, "Well you better do your best not only for tomorrow but also when we hit the one hundred meters the next day, and we want to see your name at the top of that list. I saw it when we were there and guest whose name was on top with nine hundred and sixty points, your dad followed by Dargon's father with nine hundred and forty points. You have to surpass them and get a score no one can beat." Caalin smiled, "It would be nice to score higher than the two of them, but we will have to wait and see how things go."

After everyone had cleaned up and had diner they asked Caalin to give them some more training on aiming their weapons. Caalin found an old white board and marker then drew the weapon's sights on it showing what they should be seeing when looking down the barrel of the weapon, then he drew another picture showing them what it should look like when sighting on the target. After the training everyone made their way to bed to get a good night's sleep in order to be fresh for the next day.

The next morning they made their way to breakfast then back to the range for the fifty meter firing. Once they arrived Captain Galerian informed them they had the morning to get their weapons sighted in for the range and asked Caalin to take the last spot on the range so he could step off the range once he was zeroed so they would not have to stop the firing. Caalin stood there as everyone made their way on to the range and when they were all in position he took the last spot next to the entrance. Galerian gave the command to begin firing to zero your weapons and everyone began sending rounds down range at the targets. Caalin fired five rounds all hitting the center then put his weapon down and stepped off the range as Galerian had asked. Galerian looked over at him, "You know I think if anyone can get the perfect score for weapons fire it is going to be you." Caalin just smiled, "Well, we will see."

By the end of the morning session everyone had zeroed in their weapons and broke for lunch. After lunch they returned for the qualification part on the fifty meter range, and once again Caalin fired a perfect score, and after his training with everyone the night before no one shot under seven hundred. Galerian was impressed with how well everyone had done and reminded them that the next day was the one hundred meter range and the last part of the weapons qualification. He then smile at the group, "If you all do as well as you did today you will be the first group that came through our weapons training were everyone qualified, so keep up the good work."

As they were leaving the range Galerian walked over to Caalin, "You need to be thinking about who will be doing the assault training and who will be representing your crew in the capture the flag event you can only have up to twenty people participate in both." Caalin looked over at him, "I have already been thinking about who to take, but I am waiting to see how they do tomorrow to decided where I want to place them on the team, I already have my strategy plan in my head." Galerian Laughed, "Well that just proves the stories I have heard about you, you are always thinking ahead. Well I will see you and your crew tomorrow, good luck on that perfect score."

Everyone made it back to the domicile and got cleaned up then made their way to dinner. After dinner Caalin set in the commons room looking at a map of the capture the flag area, checking out all the locations they could be ambushed and all the locations they could ambush the others. He set there staring at the map until Ang walked in, "Are you still trying to work out a plan?" Caalin replied, "Yeah I just can't detriment from which direction they will come from to capture our flag and I don't want to split everyone up to cover all the area to ambush them." Ang looked over at the map then pointed to the area right in front of what would be their tower to defend, "That looks like as good a place as any, if they get that close to our tower we should be able to stop them there." Caalin's eyes lit up and he jumped from his seat and gave Ang a big hug, "You are brilliant, that is a great idea and I think I know how to pull it off." Ang smiled, "I am glad I could be of help, but it is getting late and we have the final portion of our weapons qualification tomorrow."

Caalin got up and joined her and the two of them made their way to their rooms with Caalin giving her a quick good night kiss as he walked her to her door. The next morning it was breakfast for everyone and then back to the range, but this time it was the one hundred meter range and the last day of qualification. Caalin stopped everyone at the entrance, "Ok just because this is the last day of qualification don't forget what you have learned, breath, take aim and slowly squeezed the trigger, I have confidence in all of you so do your best."

Everyone made their way onto the range with Caalin taking the last position so he could step off the range once he was zeroed. Galerian told everyone, "Take your positions and begin firing when ready once you think you are zeroed in put your weapon down and raise your hand, we will cease fire long enough for you to step back off the range." Everyone began firing and once again after five rounds all center target Caalin stepped off the range, but what surprised Galerian was within one hour after they started everyone was zeroed in. Galerian thought for a moment, "Well this is a first but since everyone has zeroed their weapons we will go ahead with the qualification."

After a short break to allow time for the range to be set up everyone made their way back out and took their positions and the qualification began. By lunch time everything was over and everyone had qualified and to top it off everyone had qualified as sharpshooter except for Dargon, Rostrik, Jason, Clair Ssam, Ric, and Mouse who all qualified as experts. The biggest thing that happened was Caalin had scored the perfect score of one thousand points with put him at the top of the training facilities highest scores and his crew would have the most names on the list of experts.

Galerian walked over to Caalin, "Well Captain Matthews I have to say you and your crew impressed me, I never thought I would not only see someone get the maximum score but his entire crew qualified as sharpshooters or higher. I thought at least there would be a few that would only qualify as marksman but I was totally wrong." Caalin smiled, "You are absolutely right my crew impresses me, they always do their best at whatever we are doing and I am proud of every one of them." Galerian smiled, "Well you all go get some lunch and take the rest of the day off it is well deserved. You can spend the afternoon working out your strategy for the urban assault training tomorrow."

While everyone was enjoying their lunch Sara came in and made her way over to Caalin's table, "The Admiral would like to see you in his office once you have finished your meal." Caalin smiled, "Tell him I will be there in about fifteen minutes if that is ok." Sara nodded, "That is fine and I will let him know." She turned and left as Ang looked over at Caalin, "What do you think he wants to talk about this time." Caalin swallowed the food he had in his mouth, "He probably just wants to congratulate me on my qualification and talk about the upcoming events."

When Caalin finally made it over to the Admiral's Office he found out what he had told Ang was one hundred percent correct. The Admiral congratulated him and then they set down to discuss the assault training, "Tomorrow your selected team will be going through a mock village, and as you make your way through there will be targets popping up around you, your team will have to determine if the target is friend or foe before firing on it. You can only use up to twenty people for the assault, and if you hit any of the friendly targets you will have to start back over from the beginning. Plus all the target types change for every time you go through and they are not always in the same location."

He then discussed the capture the flag event, "Well lad the day after tomorrow's event involves two twenty person teams, your team will be the red team, and the first team to capture the others flag is the winner; you can use anything you have or find to help you in the process. All the weapons are stun weapons so the only thing that will happen to anyone that gets hit is that they get knock unconscious for a little while and they are out of the game." Caalin thought for a moment, "Can we use camouflage and things to block the shots from hitting us?" Admiral Madison smiled, "Yes you can even use your ability to manipulate gravity, but I really don't see how that will help you."

Admiral Madison then smiled, "Well that is all I wanted to talk to you about, you probably want to get back and start planning out your strategy for the next two days, oh and by the way when you walk back through the lobby take a look at the top qualifiers plaque, your name is right there above your father's." Caalin said his good bye and walked out of the office and as he walked through the lobby he stopped to look at the plaque.

*Weapons Qualification Top Performers*

| | |
|---|---|
| *Caalin Matthews* | *Perfect Score 1000* |
| *Thomas Matthews* | *960* |
| *Dargon Drake* | *950* |
| *Talon Drake* | *940* |
| *Rostrik Olhill* | *930* |
| *Jason Rogers* | *920* |
| *Clair Tilone* | *920* |

| | |
|---|---|
| *Ssamuel Ssallazz* | *920* |
| *Ric Harset* | *910* |
| *Mortomous Valtor* | *910* |

Caalin had a big smile on his face as he turned to leave and was quickly stopped by Dee, "I thought you might want a copy of the list of scores to take back and show the others so I brought you one." Caalin smiled at her, "Dee you're the best, thank you very much the others will be thrilled to see this." Dee smiled back, "I know they will be; I am proud of all of you myself." Caalin told her bye and took off out the door and toward their domicile to show them the list. The minute he arrived he walked over to the bulletin board in the room and pinned the list on it then turning to everyone sitting in the room shouting, "We made the list and here's the proof!" Everyone rushed up to look at it.

Caalin then took a seat and started thinking of who he wanted to do the assault training the next day, he definitely wanted everyone on the security team for it then Dargon, Ssam, Jason, Mouse, Ric, Marty, Gahe, Jon, Devlon and also Marion. He was looking at the list when Ang walked over, "What are you doing picking the people for the assault training?" Caalin looked over at her, "Well yes I am, so stop reading my mind." Ang Laughed, "I didn't have to read your mind for that, I know it is tomorrow and you can only take so many people for it, so can I see who you picked?" Caalin showed her the list and as she looked over it as she counted the people, "You only have nineteen people on the list and neither Ssophia nor I are on it." Caalin replied, "Well the two of you are medical personnel and do not need assault training and I don't need to use all twenty positions, I think I am ok with the people I selected." Ang handed the list back to him, "Well I think you made some excellent choices with your selection they all should do well." Caalin smiled, "I think they will be great at this event."

Later Caalin got the group he had selected together and went over all the information he received from the Admiral. He told them they needed to think fast to verify their target before firing on it because hitting any target of a friendly would require them to restart at the beginning again. After the briefing everyone left to go to dinner then when they returned they went to their rooms to get some rest before the next busy day.

# CHAPTER 34
||||||||||||||||||||||||||||||||||||||||||||||
# ASSAULT TRAINING

The next day everyone was up and ready to go, they made their way to breakfast and while they were eating Sara came in and let Caalin know she was there to escort him and his team to the assault training area. After breakfast the assault team told everyone they would see them later and Sara escorted them to the assault training area where they met up with Captain Galerian again.

Captain Galerian walked over to Caalin, "Well today is the assault portion of your training, this will test your ability to think fast and recognize who is the good guy and who is not, your objective here is to make it through this course with no civilian casualties." He continued, "As you make your way through targets will pop up all around you and you have to make a quick decision, are they friendly or are they the enemy, if your team shoots any of the friend targets you will have to repeat the course again and don't think you can memorized which targets pop up and where as they change for each time you go through."

Caalin thought for a moment, "How many times does it normally take a team to beat this course?" Galerian smiled, "The best team to do is was the team your father and Talon Drake were on and they did it on their third attempt." Caalin smile, "Well we need to do it in at least two or better to beat them." Galerian laughed, "Most teams take at least five or six attempts to make it through and remember this is not just based on your performance but your entire teams. Let me know when you and your team are ready to go, but remember once the target pops up you only have three seconds to fire or not fire and if you don't at least take out ninety percent of the bad guys you will have to go back through as well."

Caalin nodded, "OK, give me a few minutes to talk with my team and we will be ready." Caalin turned and walked back to his team and explained everything to them, "I think we can do this on our first run, but I need everyone doing their best. You need to make quick decisions so look for the obvious clues that tell you if they are good or bad and take your shot." After his quick briefing he let Captain Galerian know they were ready to go and they made their way to the entrance to what looked like a village with doors and windows all over the buildings plus vehicles and alleyway all along the way.

Galerian gave them the go ahead and Caalin had half his team take one side of the street while he and the others took the other side. They remained next to the buildings to give them some cover and watch the doors, windows and alleys for anything that popped up. They had not made it far when targets stared appearing and with quick decisions his team was taking out all of the bad guys and not hitting a single target of a villager.

When they reached the end of the course Captain Galerian came out to meet them, "I am impressed, I have never seen a team come through that was able to take out one hundred percent of the bad guys and not hit a single civilian in the process. Captain Matthews you have one excellent team and I am glad I got to see them in action." Caalin smile,

"You are right I do have an excellent team, just wait until tomorrow's challenge we plan on doing our best there as well." Captain Galerian smiled, "I am sure you will, I am wondering if our capture the flag team will stand a chance against yours."

Training was over and they completed the course in one run and were now on their way back to their domicile. When they walked in everyone was cheering them, it seemed the news of their completion of the course had beat them back. Ang walked over to Caalin, "I am proud of all of you, you have set a new record that I don't think anyone is going to beat." Caalin smile, "Thanks it was totally a team effort and I am proud of everyone, but we have one more test tomorrow."

# CHAPTER 35

||||||||||||||||||||||||||||||||||||||||||

# CAPTURE THE FLAG

While everyone were celebrating the assault training victory Caalin announce that he would like to have a meeting in one hour to go over the plans for the capture the flag event. He then made his way to the commons room and brought the holographic computer online to look at the area for the event. As he brought it up he could see the two towers that were close to twenty kilometers apart, with the one on the north side of the area having a blue roof and the other on the south side having a red roof.

He zoomed in on the red tower which was square at the base with covered balconies on all four sides of the second floor. The tower got narrower as it went up five floors with windows on every floor and a watch house on the top with a walk way that went all the way around. A river ran along the east side of the tower and there is a small clearing all around it.

After checking out the red tower he zoomed in on the blue one and it was a circular tower that was the same size from the bottom to the top with a guard house located on the top and a walk way all around it. It had small windows all along the walls going up the outside, and was located in a small clearing on a small piece of ground and a stream ran down and around it running from the north to the south.

While everyone was making their way into the room Caalin was setting there staring at the red tower and the area around it and finally came up with a plan. He concluded that the blue team would not attempt to attack from the west side as the river would slow them down and leave them in the open too much, so the logical attack would be from the east or north but there was too much open space to the north of the tower and they would be spotted long before they could get there. He then started putting people in positions on the hologram to determine how he wanted to guard their flag and by the time everyone were seated he had his plan to guard their tower worked out.

Everyone was seated and waiting when Caalin began to talk, "OK here is the placement of people for protecting our flag, In the tower at the top we will have Ang, Ssophia, Resrassira and Aeron, Ssophia will keep herself and Resrassira hidden until they attack, Ang and Aeron will stand watch and be available if the ground forces need them, but while they are on the walkway around the tower Ang will keep them protected using her bracelet, which I will make sure has a full charge of power.

On the ground and at the foot of the tower Mouse will keep the group hidden and protected with his stealth and force field. The ground team will be Mouse, Clair, Jason, Rostrik, Faelara, Ric, Arria, Phyla, Gahe, Jon, Marty, Marion, and Devlon and your mission is to let the enemy get as close as you can then take them out with a surprise counter attack. Dargon, Ssam and I will go after their flag and they will not know we have their flag until it is gone and we are back at our tower. They all set around going over the plan looking for any flaw that they could see when Caalin finally said, "This is not set in stone, if you need to diverge from the plan because of a change in what is happening you are welcome to do so, that is a call that I leave up to Mouse, Clair and Jason."

After the plan was hashed out for guarding the red tower Caalin asked Ssam and Dargon to stay so they could talk about what they were going to do to capture the blue flag. Caalin looked at the terrain then turned to the other two, "I think we move around and come in from the east side, Ssam can keep us out of sight went we need him too, if we run across the blue team making their way to our tower Ssam can make us invisible and we wait until they pass us by. Once we are close enough to their tower you can stand watch on the ground and Ssam can make the two of us invisible and I will fly us up to their walk that encircle the tower top and produce a shield for us by using the gravity around us, they won't know we are there until we take them out."

Caalin continued, "After we have their flag we will make our way back the way we went using Ssam to keep us out of sight if we need too. On the way back we will take out anyone that our team back at our tower may have missed but I don't think they will have any issues taking them down. Once we get back to our tower with their flag we are the winners and the event is complete." Dargon looked over at Ssam then back to Caalin, "Sounds like a solid plan to me I don't see anything wrong with it."

Later that evening at dinner Caalin ask Ang would she care to take a walk with him when they return to the dormitory and she quickly said yes. After dinner they made their way back to the dormitory and before heading off to bed the two of them took a walk out toward the landing field. Ang looked over at Caalin, "Do you want to take a flight around the base?" Caalin shook his head, "No I don't want anyone from the blue team seeing me flying, they might not know I am capable of doing that and I want to keep it a secret for now, but I promise before we leave I will take one with you." Ang smile, "That sounds great I will hold you to that promise, but I know you have something on your mind right?" Caalin stop, "Let me see your bracelet for a moment, I want to fully charge it for tomorrow, I want you to be able to produce a force field to protect everyone on that balcony with you." Ang handed the bracelet to Caalin and once he had it in his hands began forcing gravity into it until it began glowing. He then put it back on Ang's wrist, "Now I know you will be safe out there." The two of them stopped and stared up at the stars for a while then made their way back and Caalin walked her to her room and kissed her good night before heading off to bed himself.

The next morning when they arrived at the dining hall Sara and Dee were there waiting on them, Dee handed Caalin twenty red arm bands, "Your team will need to wear these on their left arm and after breakfast I will take your team to the red tower. Sara will escort the rest of your crew over to the control center where they will be able to watch everything." Caalin took the bands and walked around giving them to everyone he had selected for the event, and telling the others that Sara would be taking them to the control center so they could watch the event unfold.

After breakfast Caalin and his team followed Dee from the dining hall out to an open-air hover craft with four seats in front and two rows of bench seats running down the back of the vehicle. Dee took her seat next to the driver as Caalin and Dargon took the second row of seats right behind them while everyone else took their seats on the benches in the back. Once everyone was seated the vehicle pulled off and made its way toward the training area and the red tower. Sara led the others over to the control center and showed them to a large theater like room that had multiple screens so they could watch all the action.

Once they reached the red tower Dee looked at Caalin, "There will be a loud horn blast announcing the start of the challenge, you have one hour to get your team set up before then." Caalin thanked her and everyone on the team waved as the vehicle pulled away. Caalin looked over to Ang's team, "I want to come up to the watch tower with you and get a good look around, it may change our plans a little." He then turn to Mouse, "The rest of you wait here I want to see what area we may want to cover." He then left with Ang's team and they made their way to the top of the tower.

Once the group made it to the top Caalin walked out and around the balcony that circle the tower, "Looking this over I think they will be coming from the east as it has the most cover and they can get right up on us before we know it." He then turned to Ang and pointed out the areas she should keep a close eye on; he then had Aeron cover the other side showing him the areas that they may be able to use. Before he left the tower he took Ang's hand, "Once that horn goes off I want you to put up a shield to cover this entire area up here, I know you can do it." Ang smiled and squeezed his hand, "You know I will do my best." Caalin winked at her then made his way back down to the ground.

On the ground he got with Mouse, Clair and Jason and they all four walked around the tower looking at how close the trees were on all sides. Caalin then turn to them, "I think they will be coming from the east because it has more cover, but keep a look out in all directions just in case, and Mouse keep everyone unseen and protected until they are close enough for you to take them all out." Mouse smiled, "They won't even know what hit them." Caalin nodded, "Great once the horn goes off Dargon, Ssam and I will head up river a ways then move in their direction trying to avoid being seen."

After the hour pasted the horn blasted and Caalin, Ssam, and Dargon left the rest of the team guarding the tower. Ssophia and Resrassira disappeared on the top level with only Ang and Aeron being visible as they watched. At the bottom of the tower everyone had taken their places and vanished as well, the Admiral was in the control center and asked one of his technicians if the team on the ground moved off into the trees. The tech just replied, "I don't know sir, they were there and I looked away for a moment and they were gone."

Caalin, Ssam and Dargon had made it almost to the half way point to the blue tower when they heard some branches snapping, Ssam quickly made them disappear and Caalin put a gravity field around them just in case someone took a shot in their direction. After a moment there were four blue soldiers making their way toward the red tower. Caalin smiled then whispered, "If they think only four of them will be able to take our tower, they're in for a shock." But as soon as he said that eight more of the blue team came out of the trees behind them.

After the blue team had past them they made their way forward toward the blue tower and as they got closer Ssam made them invisible again. They came up on the east side of the blue tower and stayed as far back in the trees that they could and still get a good view of the tower. Caalin pointed out a large tree to the north of the tower that set out in the open, "Dargon you stay here, Ssam and I will make our way to that tree and once we are there I will give you a signal, then you should be able to take out one or two of them from here, once you do fall back to that old fallen tree we passed a ways back. While they are concentrating on you Ssam and I will fly up and take their flag and rendezvous with you at that tree."

Dargon agreed with the plan and took his position behind a tree, Caalin and Ssam made their way north then disappeared and reappeared behind the big tree to the north. Caalin gave Dargon a wave and Dargon fired off two shots hitting two of the eight blue team members on the tower. Ssam took hold of Caalin's arm and he flew the two of them up to the blue flag on the tower and it quickly disappeared. Caalin then flew them both in the direction of Dargon landing just in time to make him disappear before the four blue team members chasing him got to his position.

Dargon was content with standing there invisible watching them try to find his trail but Caalin reminded him that they need to make it back to win the event. With that the three of them reappeared and fired taking out the four blue team members, then they disappeared again just in case there were anyone else following them and made their way back toward their tower. Once they reached the tower they were surprised to find out that Mouse and his team had taken out all twelve of the blue team members before they got near the tower. Caalin quickly went up the tower and place the blue flag in the stand next to the red one to signal they had won the event.

They were all cheering and hugging each other when Dee arrived with the vehicle to pick them up and take them back to the control center. Once they reached the control center the rest of the crew were there to greet them cheering and hugging everyone. Admiral Madison came out to greet them, "Well Captain Matthews I have to admit that your crew has really impressed me, that was the fastest time any team has completed capture the flag and you were up against one of my best teams." Caalin smiled, "Well sir, give them my apology but they were up against my best team." The Admiral just laughed, "Well you all earned the rest of the day off, I will need you in my office tomorrow morning at 09:00 and I will sign off on your training." Caalin nodded, "I will see you in the morning sir."

After that everyone made their way back to their rooms to get cleaned up before lunch, and as they were walking back the girls started talking about going to the Base Exchange after lunch to see if there were any thing there they would like to get. After everyone had cleaned up they made their way to lunch and on the way to the dining hall Caalin whispered to Ang, "Do you want to take that flying tour of the base tonight?" Ang smiled, "Yes I would love too."

After lunch all the girls and some of the boys made their way over to the Base Exchange, but Caalin made his way back to the commons area, set down and put his feet on the table in front of him then lend back and closed his eyes. He had dozed off and was awakened by Ang when everyone returned from the Base Exchange; she wanted to show him the things she had bought. Everyone spent the afternoon talking about all the things they had done and wondering when they would be leaving. Finally it was diner time and everyone made their way to the dining hall and once they got there they found it all decorated to celebrate their completing the training. Dee and Sara were there to help them celebrate along with all the members of the blue team. The commander of the blue team kept asking Caalin how they got the flag so quickly they did not even see the people that grabbed it, it was like one moment it was there and then it was gone. Caalin just told him, "I am sorry but that has to remain a secret it is what gives us our edge over the pirates.

Finally the celebration was over and everyone made their way back to their rooms, but before they went inside Caalin grabbed Ang's hand, "I am sorry my lady but I think we have a flight scheduled for tonight." Ang Smiled. "Well what are we waiting for lets go." The two of them walked around the corner of the building, so as not to be seen, then took off into the sky. They flew out over the landing pad, over the dining hall and exchange then over the edge of the forest that led out to the capture the flag area. After about an hour the two of them returned and Caalin walked her to her room, "I always enjoy flying the skies with you." Ang kissed him on the cheek, "Not as much as I do, see you in the morning."

# CHAPTER 36

||||||||||||||||||||||||||||||||||||||||||

# RETURN TO ALLIANCE
# HEADQUARTERS

The next morning after breakfast Caalin headed over to the Admiral's office to find out what they had plan for his crew next, and once he arrived the receptionist ushered him on in. The Admiral turned to greet him, "Good Morning Captain Matthews I hope all is well with you this morning." Caalin smiled, "Yes sir everything is fine." The Admiral told him to have a seat, "Now let's get down to business, we have completed all the data updates on your ship, your computer systems have been updated and we have install new energy crystals for your drive systems." Caalin looked up, "That was a lot of work, thank you for all the help with it."

The Admiral stood up and walked around his desk, "Well lad it was nice having you and your crew here but Alliance Headquarters has asked that you return to headquarters for a new assignment. You are to meet with Admiral Nathaniel Keayan and he will brief you on the assignment." Caalin looked shocked, "Do you mean that our old headmaster is now an Admiral?" Admiral Madison laughed, "Yeah the old geezer was brought back on active duty and given a promotion on top of that." Caalin stood up, "Well sir when do we depart." The Admiral looked over at him, "As soon as you can get your gear ready a shuttle will be waiting on you to transport you and your crew back to the ship." Caalin nodded, "Well sir, I better let my crew know and we should be ready to head back to the Seeker within an hour."

Caalin started out of the office as the Admiral told Dee and Sara, "Have a shuttle ready to take Captain Matthews and his crew back to their ship, they will be ready to go within an hour." Caalin made his way back to the domicile and informed the others that they had one hour to get their things packed because a shuttle would be there to take them back to the Seeker. Within the hour everyone was packed and ready to leave, the shuttle showed up and all their bags were loaded, and they said their goodbyes to Sara and Dee then boarded the shuttle and were on their way back to their ship.

It wasn't long and they were back at port C-Twelve and walking toward the Seeker when Ang walked over to Caalin, "It will be nice to be back on the ship again, it was beginning to feel like a second home to me." Caalin smiled at her, "I feel the same way and the crew feels like an extended family as well." As they got to the ship a member of the grounds crew walked over and gave Caalin a list of all the updates that were performed, "Sir would you have your crew run checks on their systems to verify everything is working correct for you, if they are not we would like to fix any issue before you leave."

Caalin took the list and looked it over then turned to the crew member, "I will have my people run the test immediately and let you know as soon as we are done." The crewman nodded, "Thank you sir we will be waiting to hear from you." Before boarding Caalin called Mouse over and gave him part of the list, "Can you, Gahe and Jon check these items; they are all in your area?" Mouse looked at the list, "We can take care of this I will let you know once we are done with running the tests." Caalin nodded, "Great I will have the others work on the ones I have left."

Ang was waiting on him to board the ship and when Caalin caught up with her she smiled, "Already putting engineering to work I see." Caalin lowered his head, "Well to be blunt I have some items that you and the medical team need to test." Ang laughed, "Well give me our list so I will know what they changed." Caalin handed her the list of the changes they made to the medical systems, which included an update on the bodies and systems of all their crew members." Ang grabbed Caalin's arm, "Let's get on board Mr. Matthews I have a lot of work to do and you need to get to the bridge, I know there are more items there that need to be tested."

Once they were on board Ang darted off toward the medical facility to catch up with Ssophia and Sisten to run tests on the new updates. Caalin made his way to the bridge and caught up with Ssam and Ric who were already running diagnostic test on the navigation system, and Keyan and Asgaya were doing the same on the communications system. Caalin smiled, "Well since you are already ahead of me on testing the equipment here is the list of changes they made that might help, just let me know how things go."

After that Caalin made his way to the dining hall and kitchen where he handed Tehaena the list of updates they made to the kitchen and asked her to let him know when they have checked everything out properly. She smiled at him, "So far everything looks great, but we are still checking and I will have your answer soon. We are preparing for lunch so we will know if everything is working properly in no time." Caalin thanked her and made his way back to the bridge and took his seat.

Within an hour reports on all the tests were coming in, the cargo bay computers were updated and inventory was now a lot easier to track, the medical facility was operating better than before and all of the medical library had been updated, communications was improved alone with navigation and Mouse had reported that everything in engineering was in tip top shape and they were good to leave whenever he was ready. Tehaena reported that the kitchen was more efficient than it ever was and that they would be ready to serve a meal anytime someone was hungry.

Caalin contacted the ground crew and let them know that the tests were done and everything was good to go, and thanked them for their hard work. He then turned to Keyan who was still at communication, "Contact the Alliance Headquarters and let them know we are on our way back." He then turned to Ssam, "Plot our course and jump we want to get back as soon as possible I have someone I have to meet with as soon as we get there." He then contacted Mouse, "Is engineering ready, we will be pulling out soon and making a jump once we are clear of the planet." Mouse replied, "We are all good here, ready to jump whenever you are."

He then contacted the control tower and ground crews letting them know they were ready to disembark. Then he turned to Ssam, "Take us out slowly." With that all lock down cables were released and the Seeker slowly pull away from the dock and up through the atmosphere. The ship made its way into space and once they were five hundred kilometers away he gave the command, "JUMP!" With a flash and pop they were in a dimensional jump and within thirty minutes came out of the jump and were nearing Thapas the home planet of the Alliance Headquarters.

Ssam contacted the base to find out where they wanted them to land and was given docking port six zero three which was the closes docking port to the headquarters building. Ssam took the ship in slowly and once it was docked Caalin departed the ship heading to the headquarters building. Once he was at the building he told the receptionist that he was there to see Admiral Keayan, per the Admiral's request. She quickly contacted Admiral Keayan, "Sir there is a Captain Matthews here to see you, and he says you requested him?" Nathaniel replied, "Yes I did, send him right on in." She looked up at Caalin, "You can go in sir."

Caalin entered the office and Nathaniel came around his desk to greet him, "Caalin, it is great to see you again, how are you doing, and how are the others." Caalin laughed, "I am fine sir and so are the rest of your former students, but the question here is how they were able to drag you back into the Alliance and as an Admiral no less." Nathaniel looked at the boy, "I blame it all on your father, he is the one that talked me into coming back and had them sweeten it by making me an Admiral."

Caalin laughed, "Well that explains it if my dad was involved, and I am surprise that he doesn't have Dargon's dad here working with you too." Nathaniel chuckled, "I think Talon is too smart for that, besides I hear he is working with some of the resistance movements on some of the pirate held planets." He then told Caalin to have a seat, "Speaking of the resistance movements we need your help getting some weapons to a resistance group on Nabeia it is a planet in the pirate held star system Savarelia."

Caalin thought for a moment, "You want me and my crew to smuggle weapons to a resistance force on the planet Nabeia in the middle of the pirate held star system?" Nathaniel looked at him, "Is there something wrong, do you think your crew is not up to the task? I have read all the reports and I know you can do this." Caalin scratched his head, "I don't know if everyone on my ship would want to go into a pirate held star system." Nathaniel looked at him, "Talk to your crew and anyone that does not wish to go on this mission will remain here as Alliance guest, we don't want to force anyone that doesn't feel comfortable with this mission to go it. I know you are thinking about the six girls that you rescued." He then turned around and took his seat, "Talk to your crew and get back to me by tomorrow morning, we have the weapons waiting to go, and I just need your answer."

Caalin stood up, "I will talk with my crew and have an answer for you first thing tomorrow." Nathaniel smiled, "Thank you Caalin, I will wait to hear back from you." Caalin walked slowly back to his ship thinking about what Nathaniel had asked of him and his crew, once back on the ship he ask Keyan, "Please contact the entire crew and have them join me in the dining hall." He then made his way to the dining hall to wait.

Caalin entered the dining hall and Belrion walked over, "Are you going to need my people for this meeting or will it be ok if I were the only one here." Caalin looked at him, "I am sorry, but what I need to talk about concerns everyone so I will need all your people out here for the meeting." Within thirty minutes the room was full and Caalin stood up on a chair so everyone could see and hear him, "I have just come back from a meeting at Alliance Headquarters and we have a new mission, it seems that there are large pockets of resistance forces on the pirate held planets fighting back against the pirates. Lieutenant Drake's father is already working with a lot of the resistance groups, and the Alliance has asked us for our help. They want us to smuggle a load of weapons to a large group on the planet Nabeia, but it seems this planet is in the middle of a pirate held star system." He paused for a second, "As the Captain of an Alliance ship I cannot turn down this mission, but I will not take anyone with me that does not feel comfortable going into that star system. Admiral Keayan has informed me that anyone not wishing to go on this mission can remain behind as a guest of the Alliance until we return." There was another pause, "What I need to know from you is if you wish to stay behind or go with me on this mission, so if you wish to stay back please let me know by midnight so we can make arrangements, and do not worry we will not think harshly of anyone that does not think they can handle it, if it was up to me I would have turned the mission down completely rather than endanger my friends." He stepped down off the chair, "That is all you are dismissed."

Caalin quickly left the dining hall and went straight to his room so he would not have to answer any questions that may influence anyone to take the mission against their own feelings. Once in his room he lay down on his bed and stared at the ceiling wondering about how this mission would go. After a few minutes there was a knock on his door and he shouted, "It is open you may enter!" It was Ang and she walked over and took a seat on the edge of his bed, "Well Mr. Matthews I see you are torn between your mission and your crew. I am here to let you know that we all talked after you left and everyone is in agreement that if you have to take this mission then we all will take it, we are your crew and we are not going to desert you because of a mission, now get up off that bed and lets go have some lunch we have already informed the Admiral we would take the mission and they will be loading the weapons on board this afternoon."

Caalin got up off the bed and the two of them made their way back to the dining hall for lunch. They took a seat in the corner and ordered their meal and were enjoying some tea when Ssam walked over, "The Admiral sent over the data on the star system and the planet where the resistance is located, plus the rendezvous location along with the names of the resistance leaders." Ssam paused for a moment, "He also asked if we could head out first thing in the morning, but he would leave it up to you on how early." Caalin looked over at Ssam, "Pass the word to the crew we leave at 0700 tomorrow for the Savarelia Star System and the planet Nabeia, we have weapons to deliver to make for the resistance force there."

Printed in the United States
by Baker & Taylor Publisher Services